Now that the weather is [...] the sun with this month's [...] reads from Harlequin Presents!

Favorite author Lucy Monroe brings you
Bought: The Greek's Bride, the first installment
in her MEDITERRANEAN BRIDES duet. Two
billionaires are out to claim their brides—but
have they met their match? Read Sandor's story now
and Miguel's next month! Meanwhile, Miranda Lee's
The Ruthless Marriage Proposal is the sensuous
tale of a housekeeper who falls in love with her
handsome billionaire boss.

If it's a sexy sheikh you're after,
The Sultan's Virgin Bride by Sarah Morgan
has a ruthless sultan determined to have
the one woman he can't. In Kim Lawrence's
The Italian's Wedding Ultimatum an Italian's
seduction leads to passion and pregnancy!
The international theme continues with
Kept by the Spanish Billionaire by Cathy Williams,
where playboy Rafael Vives is shocked when his
mistress of the moment turns out to be much more.

In Robyn Donald's *The Blackmail Bargain*
Curt blackmails Peta, unaware that she's a penniless
virgin. And Lee Wilkinson's *Wife by Approval* is
the story of a handsome wealthy heir who needs
glamorous Valentina to secure his birthright.

Finally, there's Natalie Rivers with her debut novel,
The Kristallis Baby, where an arrogant Greek tycoon
claims his orphaned nephew—by taking virginal
Carrie's innocence and wedding her. Happy reading!

MISTRESS TO A MILLIONAIRE

*She's his in the bedroom,
but he can't buy her love...*

Showered with diamonds, draped in exquisite
lingerie, whisked around the world in the
lap of luxury...

The ultimate fantasy becomes a reality.

Live the dream with more
MISTRESS TO A MILLIONAIRE titles
by your favorite authors.

Available only in Harlequin Presents®

Cathy Williams

KEPT BY THE
SPANISH BILLIONAIRE

MISTRESS
TO A
MILLIONAIRE

HARLEQUIN®

TORONTO • NEW YORK • LONDON
AMSTERDAM • PARIS • SYDNEY • HAMBURG
STOCKHOLM • ATHENS • TOKYO • MILAN • MADRID
PRAGUE • WARSAW • BUDAPEST • AUCKLAND

ISBN-13: 978-0-373-12639-2
ISBN-10:   0-373-12639-5

KEPT BY THE SPANISH BILLIONAIRE

First North American Publication 2007.

Copyright © 2007 by Cathy Williams.

This edition published by arrangement with Harlequin Books S.A.

® and TM are trademarks of the publisher. Trademarks indicated with ® are registered in the United States Patent and Trademark Office, the Canadian Trade Marks Office and in other countries.

www.eHarlequin.com

Printed in U.S.A.

All about the author...
Cathy Williams

CATHY WILLIAMS was born in the West Indies and has been writing Harlequin romances for over fifteen years. She is a great believer in the power of perseverance as she had never written anything before and from the starting point of zero has now fulfilled her ambition to pursue this most enjoyable of careers. She would encourage any would-be writer to have faith and go for it!

She lives in the beautiful Warwickshire countryside with her husband and three children, Charlotte, Olivia and Emma. When not writing she is hard-pressed to find a moment's free time in between the millions of household chores, not to mention being a one-woman taxi service for her daughters' never-ending social lives.

She derives inspiration from the hot, lazy, tropical island of Trinidad (where she was born), from the peaceful countryside of middle England and, of course, from her many friends, who are a rich source of plots and are particularly garrulous when it comes to describing her heroes. It would seem, from their complaints that tall, dark and charismatic men are too few and far between! Her hope is to continue writing romance fiction and providing those eternal tales of love for which, she feels, we all strive.

CHAPTER ONE

RAFAEL VIVES wasn't sure whether to be amused, irritated, bored or downright enraged at the situation in which he now found himself. For a man whose *raison d'être* was his work, the mistress without rival, to be trapped in paradise for ten days on a babysitting mission was enough to make his teeth snap together in frustration. Even his twenty-four-hour accessory, his faithful laptop computer without which he would have been truly lost, could not make him forget that his stay at his mother's house in the Hamptons had not been of his choosing.

Fortunately, at the time, he had been on his New York stint, so the physical inconvenience had been lessened considerably, but, close though his office was, he had been asked, rather *told*, by his mother that he was to 'stay put and keep an eye on his brother'. He suspected that she knew him well enough to know that the minute he set foot into his office, that massive glass monster in Lower Manhattan, his mission to 'keep an eye on James, you know what he can be like' would be completely forgotten.

Her original plan had been for him to join in James's house party, a commendable reward to select employees in London and New York by way of celebrating one year's worth of substantial profit for the company.

Rafael didn't know if he or James had been more averse to the idea.

From James's point of view, one which he shared with candid horror, the idea of Rafael, as he put it, 'glowering in the corners and frightening the employees' made his blood run cold.

And, as far as Rafael was concerned, the thought of mingling with a truckload of people all day and all night, without any remission for good behaviour, was beyond the pale. In the running of the conglomerate, James was the blond-haired, blue-eyed face of advertising campaigns, and he, Rafael, the brains and horsepower that drove the company.

The symbiotic relationship worked and Eva, their mother, was forced to concede to their reluctantly agreed concession.

James would host the party at the house, a sprawling beach mansion poised on three acres of land and overlooking the spectacular beauty of prime Hamptons beach.

Rafael, from the peace and seclusion of a guest cottage in the grounds, would oversee things, ensuring that neither the music nor the fun and frolics got out of hand.

The last time James had hosted a party at the house, neighbours had complained and that was quite something considering how far away the nearest neighbour lived.

Of course, as Rafael had pointed out to his mother in an attempt to divert her from her insistence on his presence at the event, that had been two years ago and the party had been laid on for James's personal friends, all in their early to mid twenties, rather than employees of the company, but his objections had been in vain. Eva Lee still shuddered at the memory of the fiasco and the inevitable all round apologies to her friends at the East Hampton Improvement Society.

So here he was now, one day into his Big Brother role and already itching to get back to the cut and thrust of what he knew and loved.

But at least, he conceded, the scenery was magnificent, forced as he was to contemplate it. It briefly, though only briefly, occurred to him that he didn't visit the place often enough. The idyllic days of youth spent at the then family home had gradually tapered off to the occasional visits in between his university studies and thirst for foreign travel. And then his working life had begun in earnest, first operating independently at one of the biggest broking houses in the world and thereafter at the helm of the family company, following the untimely death of his stepfather, and James's dad.

From there on in, time and the years had galloped away, leaving him now to ruminate as he stared at the stunningly beautiful and dipping sunset at the possibility that he would wake up one day only to find himself a middle-aged man married to a company.

Rafael frowned grimly and sipped the whisky and soda he had prepared for himself. Introspection was not a pastime he indulged. He had always been goal-oriented and had seldom questioned the unutterable direction of his plans.

He wasn't about to start now.

On the drift of the breeze, he could hear the faraway sounds of forty-odd people having a good time.

It wasn't too hard to picture the scene. James, naturally, would be in the thick of it. Pre-dinner drinks would be on the go and, of course, with an army of staff requisitioned to ease the strain of actually having to do very much of a practical nature, there would be no headaches over what to cook for everyone to eat or even when to top up the empty glass. The finest wine would be accompanied by the finest food and everything would be served by the most reliable and efficient of staff that money could buy.

Spirits would be merry, indiscretions would doubtless abound, especially considering that employees on either side of the Atlantic would be meeting for the first time, without the annoying presence of spouses or partners to cramp the merriment. In the morning hangovers would probably be rampant, but at least for the while some very thorough guilt-free drinking would be done. Of that Rafael was utterly sure. And never mind the jet lag.

He downed his drink and breathed a hearty sigh of relief that he was to be spared the fun and games.

He really didn't know any of the people who had been invited to the bash. James had told him that the accountants and the managers and the marketing crew, who always basked in the limelight when it came to credit and applause for company profits, would be given a bonus, but the *'forgotten crew'* would glory in their once-in-a-lifetime experience of the East End of New York's Long Island. Rafael's mind had boggled at the speculation of what his brother meant by the 'forgotten crew', although he had to admit that the sentiment was in the right place. Rewards should not be confined to the obvious but should filter down the line into the pockets of those whose profiles were less highly visible.

As he stood on the small wooden porch, staring out to the ocean, Rafael mused on how vastly different he was to his half-brother. They might well have been strangers, so great was the chasm between them as far as their personal tastes in friends, women and lifestyles were concerned.

He was idly speculating on how two people who shared at least some of the same DNA code could be so wildly different when he spotted something out of the corner of his eye. Something or someone. A faint rustling amongst the lush, perfectly landscaped vegetation that signified a *presence*.

And a *presence* could only mean one thing. A party-goer, in the heat of the moment and with the wine flowing like a fountain, had failed to realise that he had strayed out of bounds.

Rafael carefully put his glass down and turned towards the direction of the rustling. The light might be fading, but he wasn't blind and the bimbo trying to tiptoe away from the scene of the crime must have had all of one brain cell to imagine that he couldn't see her. And he could. Blonde hair, of course. Faded cut-off jeans worn very tight. Naturally. Cropped top with obligatory slither of stomach exposed. In other words, just the sort of woman Rafael found deeply unappealing.

'Hey, you!'

Lord, his voice ricocheted around Amy and she gave a little startled yelp as she turned tail to flee. One glance at the man, all shadow and substance at the same time, was enough to warn her that, whoever the hell he was, he wasn't the sort to chuckle over the fact that she was probably trespassing on his property.

Not that it was easy to tell where James Lee's property began and ended.

The place was just so *big!* Even with a severe case of jet lag kicking in, it was still impossible to miss the fact that 'the family house' stopped only a few polite centimetres short of being a hotel. And the grounds! Succulently tempting. Even with her body clock warning her that it might be time to head for her bedroom, the verdant lawns with their masterfully landscaped grounds had egged her on, tempting her to explore just for a little while.

Hence the fact that she was now trying to dodge a giant of a man who seemed to be rapidly closing ground between them.

She was barely aware of his stealthy movement towards her and was, in fact, breathing a sigh of relief that she had escaped, when a hand closed over her shoulder, yanking her to a sudden, painful halt, before swinging her around so that she was forced to look up…and up…until she was staring into the most forbidding face she had ever seen in her life. Black eyes glared down at her from a face that was all disturbing angles and shadows. His mouth was a thinly drawn line of suppressed anger. Amy's breath caught in her throat as she stared up at him, her eyes widening as her brain rapidly went through the various possibilities for danger that were confronting her.

Fortunately for Amy, danger, the unknown and certainly threatening oversized strangers were not things that could keep her exuberant nature suppressed for too long.

'Who the hell are you?'

'What the hell do you think you're doing here?'

They spoke at the same time, glaring at each other with equal ferocity, until Amy slapped his hand off her shoulders and stepped back, her blue eyes spitting fire.

'I asked you first!' Amy decided to go on the immediate attack because, for once, her vocabulary was threatening to let her down when she needed it most. She rubbed her shoulder meaningfully, every inch of her five-foot-three frame emanating anger.

Rafael took a deep breath and summoned up the formidable self control that had made him such a powerful contender in the world of high finance. He turned his back and began walking away, towards the house, leaving the wretched blonde to stew in her own pathetic discomfort, even though every fibre in his being wanted to prolong the confrontation so that he could put her soundly in her place.

'Hey! Where do you think you're going, mister?'

Rafael turned around and stared at the diminutive figure that hadn't budged from where he had left her. This time, her hands were planted firmly on her hips. The breeze, he could see, was wreaking havoc with the curly fair hair, blowing it this way and that. The cropped top had ridden up a little higher and there was slightly more of that slither of stomach visible.

In every way, shape and form, this woman conformed to

his brother's idea of the perfect woman, from the obvious clothing to the flyaway blonde hair. The only variation on the theme seemed to be that this particular model didn't have the requisite big breasts.

'I beg your pardon?' Rafael said with icy politeness, hardly believing his ears.

'You heard me!' Amy took a couple of steps forward. 'Who the heck are you and what do you think you're doing on James Lee's property?'

'Oh, good God. A madwoman. I suppose you're a member of his guest list up at the big house and you're a little worse for wear.' Rafael checked his watch. 'Pretty good going considering you really haven't been here that long.' He gave a short, sarcastic little laugh that made the blood rush to Amy's head.

'How *dare* you?'

She had taken a few steps closer to him. Now, with the light from the porch spilling onto her, Rafael could see that the cute little figure, minus the large breasts, was accompanied by a face that might have passed for just another pretty one were it not for the lively expression on it. He had an idea that this woman was not backward when it came to self-expression. Loud mouthed and brash, he assumed, with distaste.

As if to cement the unfortunate impression, Amy glared at him. 'Does James know that you're here? Ha! I'll bet he doesn't! I know *for a fact* that he doesn't use this place very often so I'm sure he'd be overjoyed to know that there's a squatter on the grounds!'

'Squatter?' Rafael gave a roar of laughter.

'You heard me. A squatter!' Well, he didn't exactly look like one, but, then again, he certainly didn't look like one of the people James would normally mix with. Of which she was not exactly one, but she sure as heck knew what they were like because she saw them often enough in the director's restaurant, where she worked behind the lines, providing high-quality food for the high-quality executives, and, sometimes after hours, for James's personal entourage, glamorous women and playboy men who occasionally had a bite to eat in the boardroom before heading out to some trendy London night spot.

Of course, none of the directors knew that James was the unofficial recipient of Amy's catering skills. For the past year and a half that had been their little secret and one that was so *James* with his winning, risqué ways, his charming disregard for convention except when it suited him.

Wasn't that why she had taken to daydreaming shamelessly about him over time? Oh, he was so much more than just a good-looking face and a moneyed background!

Amy surfaced from her distracting thoughts to find the man, now recovered from his laughing fit, eyeing her coldly.

'I am not a *squatter.* In fact, I've never heard such a ridiculous suggestion in my life.'

'Then who *are* you?'

'Someone who isn't about to stand around here and have a pointless discussion with some woman who's the worse for wear.'

'I am *not* the worse for wear!'

'Well, you're certainly behaving like you are.' Rafael's voice dripped contempt. Some men liked shrieking women, but he wasn't one of them. He liked them refined, elegant, composed. His expression hardened. 'And I have no desire to conduct a conversation with a fishwife.'

Amy gasped. His lack of common courtesy was somehow shocking, especially, she thought belatedly, considering he was talking to a guest of the man on whose grounds he had apparently set up camp. Legally or illegally, she had yet to find out.

Yet again he had turned his back on her and was striding

towards the house. He couldn't possibly be oblivious to her presence because she was hardly trying to be silent, but he certainly wasn't spinning round to continue the sparring match.

In fact, she hopped onto the covered wooden porch at roughly the same time as he swung through the front door and without a backward glance slammed it firmly in her face.

As expected, it wasn't long before Rafael heard the woman banging on the door. At this rate, between her uncontrolled shrieking and the unholy racket she was now making, the neighbours would be reporting *him!*

He went very close to the door, close enough so that he didn't actually have to raise his voice very much to be heard. 'Go away. You're making a fool of yourself. I don't much give a damn whether you're drunk or not but I don't have time for women who think they can get their own way by screaming and yelling. So run along to where the fun is, stock up on a bit more booze and then collapse, like everyone else, into bed.'

'If you don't tell me who you are I'm going to have to report you to James.' Amy lowered her voice to match his, although she wasn't quite sure whether she sounded as cold and forbidding as he did. She just hoped that she didn't sound like a petulant child who would resort to *telling* because the temper tantrum hadn't worked.

'I'm sober enough to know that you might not have permission to be on these grounds.' In fact, she hadn't drunk anything at all, despite the abundance of alcohol on offer. All manner of sightseeing tours had been laid on for them to enjoy and she wasn't about to miss a single one of them because of a hangover. Nor was she about to squander any precious moments she could spend in James's company by having unnecessary lie-ins.

It worked. To her astonishment. The man opened the door, glared at her and informed her that she could come inside.

For the first time, with the lights in the room switched on, she saw him properly. He was tall and she had been right about the raven-black hair. In fact the only thing she had missed and that was becoming patently clear was that he was incredibly, undeniably sexy. Not sexy in a magazine centrefold kind of way, but sexy in a powerful, brooding, rough-edged kind of way. It almost took her breath away, then she stared around her, curiosity temporarily silencing her.

The house might have been small but it was far from shabby. The rich patina of wooden flooring glistened, invited the eye to linger over the comfortable sitting area, which was dominated by a large, modern-style fireplace, coaxed it into straying just a bit further to glimpse a high-tech kitchen, then up a few short stairs to where, presumably, the bedrooms were.

'Not bad for a squatter,' she said, adding, 'ha, ha,' when he frowned at her. 'Look, I'm sorry if you're suffering a severe case of wounded pride because I called you a squatter, but I was a little shocked to find somebody out here, holed up miles away from the house.'

Rafael stared at her, fascinated against his will. Not only did she appear to have no braking mechanism controlling what came out of her mouth, but she was now wandering through the house as if she really were a guest, rather than an intruder who had managed to wrangle her way in by dint of threat.

The fact of the matter was that Rafael did not want his presence on the grounds to be an open secret. He genuinely didn't want to be a dampener on proceedings, nor did he want to feel obliged to join in the fun. He had his own idea of fun. Dinner with friends, intimate jazz clubs with like-minded women. Certainly not drinking till dawn around a pool at the family mansion in the Hamptons with a random selection of people he didn't know from Adam but was pretty sure he wouldn't particularly like. Just as he didn't particularly care for the woman standing in front of him, making no pretence at covering up her nosiness.

'So if you're not a squatter, then *who are you*?'

I just own the company you work for, Rafael was tempted to inform her. It didn't surprise him that the woman had failed to recognise him. As she was a member of the *'forgotten crew'*, he suspected that whatever job she did would be fairly low profile and definitely out of sight. It had to be said that he was also rarely in London, choosing to oversee things from New York, and judging from her accent she was definitely one hundred per cent Londoner.

'I'm the...gardener,' Rafael improvised.

'And you live *here?*'

'Where else would you expect me to live?'

'In a small, average house on a small, average estate somewhere fairly close by...like any other normal gardener...'

'In case it missed you, this isn't exactly a small, normal garden. It's a full-time job, hence my residence on the grounds.'

'And your staff come in every day to mow the lawns...' That made a bit more sense because she couldn't really picture him pushing a mower himself. He didn't look the type, although if his body was anything to go by he had no end of muscular brawn at his disposal. No, he definitely looked more the sort to give orders and, furthermore, to *enjoy* giving orders. She felt immediate sympathy for his absent staff.

'Mow the lawns...keep the gardens in check...do whatever needs doing...'

'And you control the whip.' It was said in a light-hearted tone of voice, but of course he refused to crack a smile, prompting her to enquire whether a lack of a sense of humour was part of his job description.

Amy liked people with a sense of fun. She came from a sprawling family of six children and, like most children from large families, she had never had much experience with the concept of privacy. She enjoyed sharing. She laughed easily. She liked to have a good time. It was one of the many things about James that she found so attractive. His wicked sense of fun.

This man on the other hand was the epitome of grim-faced seriousness.

'Are you always so…*serious*?' she asked, looking at him, but not for too long because he really *was* very sexy indeed, if you went for the brooding kind of man. Which she didn't.

Rafael, unaccustomed as he was to being spoken to like this, was temporarily lost for words and in the brief silence Amy carried on blithely.

'I mean…what have you got to be grim about? You live in a fantastic place, paid for by your employer. And I bet you also have lots of other perks that go with the house.'

'Perks?'

'Sure.' She tabulated them on her fingers, one at a time. 'Car. Hiding in a garage somewhere, I expect, and probably not any old banger. Pension plan. End-of-year bonuses. Am I right?' The tiredness that had seen her stepping out of the house for a breath of fresh air, then wandering much further than she had intended, seemed to have disappeared.

'I can tell from your silence that I'm right!' she said triumphantly. 'Lucky old you.'

Rafael did not intend to be drawn into any conversation with a dippy blonde who had managed to stray out of her depth. He opened his mouth to tell her politely, but firmly, that it was time for her to leave.

'Why do you say that?' he heard himself ask and she shot him a wide, infectious grin.

'Because I do a similar sort of thing and I certainly don't have the great perks that you do.'

'You're a…gardener?'

'Caterer.'

'And catering is similar to gardening?'

'Well, we both work with our hands and are creative with it…so, yes…pretty much, wouldn't you agree?'

'I can't say that there's anything creative about gardening.'

Amy looked at him in surprise. Again, she was struck by the force of his physical presence, which, she told herself with a little inner laugh, was just silly. 'Then why do you do it?'

Rafael gave an impatient shrug and ran his fingers through his hair. 'Look. I've humoured you by letting you in and you now know why I'm here. So time for you to go and I'd appreciate it if you could keep my presence here to yourself.'

'Because…?'

'Because I don't want to be overrun by James's house guests when I'm trying to do my job.'

'You're on first names with your *boss*? Hmm.' She thought about it for a few seconds, then her face softened. 'Not surprising really.'

'What's not surprising?' Rafael frowned. 'No. Forget I said that. Have a good time here. I'm sure you will. It's a beautiful place. Lots to do and explore if you choose to leave the house and pool.'

He began walking towards the door, not giving her time to continue with her relentless chatter.

'Do you realise we haven't even exchanged names?' Amy said, sticking out her hand. 'I'm Amy.'

'Why should we have exchanged names?' He pulled open the door and stood back, sticking one hand in the pocket of his cream Bermuda shorts.

Even at night, the temperatures meant that shorts and tee shirts could be comfortably worn. For Rafael, who lived most of his life in his tailored, handmade suits, a pair of shorts and a faded tee shirt constituted the highest form of luxury.

'That's *very* rude.' Amy withdrew her hand and pulled herself up so that she could fix him with a gimlet eye.

'*What's* very rude? You know what? I'm not really all that interested anyway.' Outside, in the balmy air, a very gentle breeze lifted the breathtakingly blonde curls and made them dance.

'I don't care whether you're interested or not! I'm going to tell you anyway! It's *rude* to look at someone as though they've got a contagious disease when they're doing nothing more than attempting to introduce themselves! If you don't want to tell me your name, then that's fine! It's no skin off my nose! It's not as though I'm—'

'Rafael.'

'I beg your pardon?'

'Rafael. My name is Rafael Vives.' He held out his hand and as Amy took it she felt a strange quiver of awareness dart its way through her body like a sudden, unexpected jolt of electricity, then the feeling was gone.

'I'm Amy.' As quickly as her temper had surfaced, it was gone. Anger was something she had never been able to hold onto for very long. 'Rafael…unusual name… Is it…what? Italian?'

'Spanish,' Rafael said abruptly. 'Will you be able to find your way back to the house?'

'Oh, yes? How did a Spanish gardener come to be working in America?' She fished into a pocket, pulled out an elastic band and expertly tied her hair back into a loose pony tail.

'Buy yourself a potted history guide book, speed read it and you'll discover how we Spaniards managed to find our way over here. Now off you go.'

'You're very arrogant, aren't you?'

'Yes. Yes, I am, and now that we've cleared that up you can be on your way.'

To his relief she took the hint and for a few seconds he watched her head off, pause, glance around her, head off, but this time in a different direction. Her antics would have been amusing had he not known that sooner or later he would have to point her in the right direction. The grounds to the house were extensive and the verdant lawns were interspersed with grassy dunes and dense trees. There was even a tiered pond with a waterfall set in richly colourful gardens. When you knew the property, you knew easily how to find your way around, but to the uninitiated it could be bewildering, especially in the dark. And the guest cottage, which had been indeed built to house the head of the domestic staff when the house had been fully utilised, was not easy to find.

With a deeply impatient sigh, Rafael fetched the key, slammed the door behind him and caught up with her as she veered off on her fourth aborted attempt to locate the right way back.

He circled his hand around her arm and ushered her in the opposite direction.

'Good God, woman! Where's your sense of direction?'

'I would have found my way eventually! And do you mind letting me go? You're not a policeman and I'm not under arrest!'

'I'm just making sure that I get you off my property!'

'*Your* property? That's a bit rich considering you're only the gardener! I know the gardens are *unusually big* so you must be an *unusually important* gardener, but hey! You're just still a gardener!'

'Do you ever shut up?' Rafael muttered under his breath.

'Are you ever polite?' He still had his hand wrapped around her arm like a steel clamp and Amy had given up on trying to shake him off. 'It's not my fault these grounds are so *big*! Well, actually, it *is* kind of my fault. I suppose I could have stayed put at the house with everyone else.'

'Yes. That you could have done. Why didn't you?' She was very slight. Her arm felt fragile in his hand. He imagined that if he were to ever pick her up, she wouldn't weigh a thing. He released her and shoved his hands in his pockets.

'I was tired.' She shrugged. 'Normally I'm up for any party but I just fancied a little bit of time on my own.'

'There was a *party* going on when you left?' Rafael's ears pricked up. 'What kind of party?'

'Oh, the usual. Loud music. People passing out in the flower beds. Skinny-dipping in the pool.'

Rafael spun her around to face him. 'You're kidding, aren't you? I would have heard if there was loud music. It's a still night.'

Amy looked up at him in astonishment and then burst out laughing. 'Of course there was no party, Mr Gardener! I just meant that, after the "getting to know you" over the cocktails, I decided that a little walk in the garden might wake me up! It was all perfectly civilised. The flower beds are all still intact, in case that was what you were worried about.'

'Of course I wasn't worried about the damned flower beds!'

'Then you don't take your job as seriously as you should!' Amy chided teasingly. 'Anyway, why on earth should you care whether James has a party up at the house or not? It's not really your business, is it?'

'If you peer into the distance you can see the lights of the house. Follow them.'

'You mean you won't do the gentlemanly thing and walk me to the front door? And before you start glowering, it was just a joke. Do you ever get lonely?'

'I beg your pardon?'

'Do you ever get lonely? You know…stuck up there on your own from dawn to dusk…'

'What makes you think that I'm stuck there on my own?' Rafael couldn't resist asking. Even without benefit of light, he could see the embarrassed surprise on her face. 'Don't you think that there's a woman who wouldn't mind helping while away the occasional lonely night?' he drawled.

Amy could feel hot colour flood her cheeks as she struggled to find a suitably composed reply. Eventually she stammered, clearing her throat, 'Well, you just seemed to overreact to the idea of a party, so I thought that maybe…perhaps you…'

'Perhaps I was a complete bore who enjoyed nothing more than pruning the rose bushes while pouring scorn on other people's good times?'

'No, of course not!'

'I know how to enjoy myself, little Amy.'

The way he said that sent shivers running up and down her spine. From somewhere, she managed to dredge up the image of James, smiling, blond-haired James with his teasing blue eyes and ready grin, and just about managed to ward off the more disturbing one of Rafael the arrogant gardener in bed with a woman who wanted to help him while away a lonely night.

'I just don't happen to be a party animal. Drinking myself into a stupor has never held much appeal.'

Rescued from her sudden, acute embarrassment and overactive imagination, Amy was happy to be diverted back to her healthy opinion of him as an arrogant bore.

'No, I could tell.' His body language was letting her know in no uncertain terms that he couldn't particularly care less what she thought of him, but Amy couldn't seem to let it go. Arrogant bore or not, there was something curiously fascinating about him. 'You've probably never been to a really good party' she said, consolingly. 'It's not all about drinking yourself into a stupor. It's about good company and good music and lots of dancing.'

She grinned at him, amused at his expression of distaste. 'Which bit of that do you find off-putting?'

'The bit that reeks of excess,' Rafael told her coolly.

'Which is where you're in danger of going unless you clear off. I'm sure, as the party animal that you are, you don't set much store on privacy, but I do and I would appreciate it if you respected that and stayed away from my property. Think you can understand that?'

Amy felt sudden tears of hurt prick the backs of her eyes and she nodded. 'I'm sorry,' she said in a small voice, which made him feel like a monster.

Rafael gave her a curt nod and turned away. It was bad enough having to take time out when there were a million things that urgently needed doing without finding his precious time further usurped by a trail of unwanted explorers making the most of their bonus week off.

When he eventually turned around to make sure that she was walking in the right direction, she had disappeared.

CHAPTER TWO

THINGS had been laid on.

Amy woke early the following morning, drifted downstairs and discovered, to her surprise considering James's casual personality, that their days had been mapped out and planned with military efficiency.

Several others were likewise up and in the dining room, which had been laid out for breakfast buffet style.

On one wall was a large notice board indicating the activities in store for them that day, should they wish to avail themselves of it.

From behind her, Claire, her closest friend at the house, tapped her on the shoulder and giggled something about how the other half lived and that they should tuck into breakfast because not having to prepare it themselves was a luxury that wouldn't rear its head again in a hurry.

'Darn right!' Amy laughed back, easily slipping into the fun-loving girl her friends all knew and appreciated. It wasn't long before she had joined some of the others, happily allowing herself to be swept up in the excitement of planning which events they were going to try out later on.

Of course, there was always the option of staying put, which some of them intended to do, but there would also be an opportunity to go kayaking and canoeing. For the lazier of them, fishing was an option, as well as a chance to explore some of the beaches, which would involve picnics and swimming.

Amy wondered which, if any, James would be going to. He was nowhere to be seen, but when he did appear she intended to get herself noticed in a way she had yet to do.

Thus far, she had always been the very good caterer at work, always decked out in her boring white outfit and caterer's hat. It was the least sexy outfit possible to don. Not that Amy considered herself to be the centrefold of a magazine, but she had a friendly personality and many people had told her that she was quite cute.

Well, cute could work. She had tied her hair back into two braids that reached just past her shoulders, a touch-and-go hairstyle as far as attracting the opposite sex went but very practical in hot weather. Her blue and white top was jaunty and her jeans were, she thought, just the right side of trendy. Very skinny-fitting and just right with the flat, beaded silver shoes that she could kick off if need be or walk a hundred miles if she had to.

'Which tour do you think he's going to be on?' she whispered to Claire, as soon as they had sat down in front of plates that were groaning with a ridiculous amount of food. 'I've dressed the part.' She thought, briefly and unexpectedly, of the arrogant gardener she had bumped into the previous night. She imagined he would give her one of those ice-cold looks were he to see her in her get-up. For a second she was tempted to let Claire into the little secret, but she held her tongue, remembering the way he had told her to keep his presence on the ground to herself.

'What part?' Claire grinned. She was as plump and dark as Amy was fair and slender, but they had hit it off the minute they had met two years previously and were still the best of friends.

'The part that's not covered up in a white uniform with neat white plimsolls and a hairnet. A hairnet! Do you think he'll notice me?'

'He *always* notices you,' Claire said, prompted into automatic support.

'Yes, well. He chats and laughs but he does that with *everyone*!' She skewered a piece of fresh pineapple on her fork, inspected it and popped it into her mouth. 'I wonder which exciting little tour he'll be on.'

Claire watched her friend drift off into some pleasant daydream land and bit back the instinct to protect her from hurt by telling her how she really felt—that James liked her well enough but that was as far as it went. She was pretty sure that he really would never actually have a relationship with someone who worked for him anyway, because wouldn't that be against some company law? But even if he could have, he joked with her the way a guy joked with a woman he thought of as a mate. She should know. That had been her fate for long enough!

'Just enjoy yourself, Ames, and forget about James. He'll be at the barbecue tonight anyway!'

And as it turned out the tight-fitting jeans and the jaunty top had been in vain. James had gone off fishing for the day, bonding with some of the junior lads in the marketing department. The outfit, furthermore, had been a serious impediment when it came to kayaking and by the time four o'clock rolled round and they were all trooping wearily back to the house Amy was more than a little disconsolate.

What was she doing? She was twenty-four years old and was committing the unforgivable sin of throwing herself at someone with the desperation of an ageing spinster under threat of being left on the shelf! It was ridiculous. *She* was ridiculous!

She almost believed it, almost figured that she had got her emotions under control, when she spotted him later that night, standing outside in the garden, drink in one hand, laughing with a little group of people around him, and then her heart fluttered a bit and she drew in her breath and headed in his direction.

The barbecue was kicking off in jolly style. Wine was being served and a selection of exquisite canapés, just substantial enough to take the edge off the alcohol before food, was brought out.

James spotted her weaving her way in his direction and for a second or two he hesitated, then there he was, breaking away from the group and coming towards her.

Actually, Amy could scarcely believe her eyes. In fact, she turned around to see if there was anyone behind her towards whom he could be heading.

When she looked back round he was right there, in front of her, his blond hair rumpled, his whole look adorably preppie. He gave her a crooked smile and she smiled back happily.

'I didn't recognise you.' He held her hand, stepped back and made her do an impromptu twirl, then he gave a long, low wolf-whistle.

'Is that a good thing or a bad thing?' Amy said, cheeks pink. She couldn't quite make her voice sound husky, but she gave him the best flirty look at her disposal, all fluttering eyelashes and coy smile.

'A *very* good thing!' He laughed. 'The skirt suits you. In fact, your legs suit you. Very nice legs.'

'Hmm. All two of them!' She felt rather pleased now that she had made the effort to wear the red and black floaty skirt she had brought over, even though the barbecue was being held in the garden so dressing up wasn't *de rigueur.* The strappy red top made her feel wonderfully feminine.

'Tell me what you did today,' he said, eyes on her as he polished off his drink and signalled to a waiter for a refill without actually turning around.

Amy told him, skipping out certain unfortunate details, such as nearly tipping over their kayak in an attempt to swap places with Justin and getting her jeans soaked to the thighs because she should have worn shorts like everyone else, not to mention the little fact that her glorious bead shoes were now drying on her window ledge and would probably never be the same again. He seemed amused enough at her rendition of the day's events.

The one thing she omitted to tell him was about her encounter with his gardener. Why spoil the moment? From feeling a little downbeat, she had bounced right back to her cheerful self, basking in the once-in-a-lifetime experience of being the centre of James's attention.

Out of the corner of her eye, she could see Claire grinning like a hyena, and Amy made sure to angle her body away from her friend. She might be crazy about James, but she would die a thousand deaths if he ever discovered that, and Claire with her antics was hardly being the soul of subtle discretion.

But already she could sense that James was ready to move on, to circulate, and she looked wistfully at his departing back as he reached for another glass of wine and headed off, always solicitous when it came to involving each and every one of his guests.

For a few seconds, it dawned on her that those few moments of snatched time during which he had complimented her, actually *looked at her,* really amounted to not very much, but she quickly brushed aside that pessimistic train of thought.

'I think,' she told Claire later, when food had been eaten and the assembled crowd had moved on to the sort of abandoned dancing that only alcohol could induce, 'that I'm making headway.'

'Oh, I don't know, Ames…' James seemed to have disappeared from the scene, although it was hard to tell because it was dark and there were so many people all over the place.

'He asked me what I thought of the food.'

'What did you say?'

'Told him it wasn't a patch on mine.'

'You never!'

'Yup.'

'Bad move. Maybe he'll sack his caterers here and rope you in to do the cooking.'

They giggled, enjoying the novelty of being far from familiar shores in a setting they would never again experience.

Amy drained her glass of wine and decided that she would try and locate the errant James.

It had gone eleven and the party, subdued considered the amount of alcohol on offer, was still going strong. No one, in fact, had gone to bed yet as far as she could see, and Amy wasn't going to be the first. The American crowd, who were either staying at a local hotel or else returning to their own homes, would be the first to go. She imagined that, with the crowd diminished, she might yet find another opportunity to chat to James, to let him see her in a different light. Hopefully not a sozzled light. However much Amy enjoyed having a good time, she knew when to stop drinking. Despite, and she thought once again of the gardener and his high-handed, self-righteous, priggish judgements, what certain people might think.

But still… It was fun mingling and fun being asked to dance, and if her glass continued to be topped up despite her feeble attempts at shaking her head whenever one of the waiters poled along, then why shouldn't she get into the spirit of things?

Besides, as the evening wore on the wine was doing a very good job of keeping her maudlin thoughts at bay. Having a crush on the boss was the oldest, saddest story in the book. If her brothers ever found out, she didn't know which of the three of them would die laughing first, and she didn't think her sisters would be too full of tea and sympathy either. She was a pretty outgoing sort and had had her fair share of boyfriends yet here she was, in the most impossibly stunning location in the world, surrounded by lots of lively people roughly her own age, and what was she doing? Ferreting around to see if she could spot a man who didn't give her the time of day.

When she thought like that, her spirits dipped once more. Yet again, her outfit was going to be wasted. She had visions of thousands of outfits being bought and wasted in her attempts to steal James's attention.

On that thought, she set down her wineglass and drifted away from the party and the house. Away from the crowds, the glaring realisation that she wasn't having the good time she should have been hit her and Amy began to feel a little more upbeat. In a minute she knew that her instinct to make the best out of any situation would surface and she would be fine. She would sit a while and let Nature and her naturally buoyant personality take their course.

She quietly hived off towards the expertly landscaped wooded area, moving steadily away from the noise of the party.

It was late but not particularly cool and the fresh air was doing wonders for her fuzzy head. Indeed, her spirits were on the up when she was aware of movement in a little clearing in the trees. Goodness only knew how they had managed to do it, but the copse was cleverly interspersed with small benches that had been fashioned roughly out of gnarled tree trunks, so that at first glance they looked like part of the natural scenery. Amy went into immediate stealthy mode and didn't even bother to try and fight her curiosity.

She peered, eventually making out who the two people on the bench were. It was dark, but not completely. Moonlight cast a dull, ephemeral light and as the couple moved apart for a few seconds she saw them clearly. The woman she didn't recognise. Long, poker-straight hair, very fair skin and a body that was in a state of semi undress.

The man…well, the man…

She felt a tide of nausea rise up her throat and she took a couple of steps backwards, standing perfectly still when a twig snapped under her foot, but the couple were too engrossed in one another to hear the snapping of any twig. In fact, they would probably have been deaf to an approaching intercity train. When he pulled the woman so that she could straddle him, Amy fled.

Her heart was pounding. She tried hard to be quiet, but after five minutes the need to get as far away from the sight of James wrapped around a woman was so great that she stopped giving a damn how much noise she made.

She hit some part of the gardens but she wasn't sure which part because she could no longer see the house, nor could she hear the strains of the music.

She was sharing a bedroom with Claire, who had turned in a while before. Who was going to miss her?

Amy willed herself to stop running and to get her breathing under control. Okay, here were the facts. The man she was mad about was involved with someone else. She was also lost. The first she would have to put on hold until she could cry about it later. The second she would have to sort out right away or else risk spending the night somewhere in the acres of estate with only her thoughts for company.

With typical pluckiness, Amy drew in a deep breath and did what every good Girl Guide book would suggest at a time like this. She looked for a tall tree. Not too hard. Actually, they *all* looked pretty tall. Enormous, in fact, to someone pretty short, but, drawing in a deep breath, she kicked off her useless strappy sandals, and yet again wished she were decked out in something more suitable—talk about getting her dress code all wrong—and began to climb.

She got high enough to panic but not nearly high enough to see where the house was, at which point she threw caution to the winds and began yelling her head off.

When she next got up the courage to look down, it was to see the unmistakable shape of the gardener staring up at her. Of course, it *would* be the gardener.

'I'm stuck!'

'Why are you up a tree?' Rafael felt his lips twitch. That blonde tangle of hair announced its owner with a glaring lack of subtlety.

'Never mind that! You need to get me down!'

'Sorry, but I don't hear you using that special little word.'

'Now's not the time for games!'

'Always time to be polite.'

'You're a fine one to talk,' Amy yelled down, 'considering your rudeness the last time we met!' She felt her grip on the tree branch get precariously unsteady and ordered him to go and fetch a ladder *instantly*! *Please*!

'There's no ladder at the cottage. Hang on and I'll get you down!'

Amy closed her eyes. She was aware of him climbing up the tree, skilfully manoeuvring the trunk and the branches. She had never felt more of an idiot in her life. Her skirt was everywhere. Floaty was fine at a party but not so fine when it came to shinning up a tree and having to be ignominiously fetched down like a stray cat.

And Lord only knew what it was doing as he coaxed and aided her down, holding onto her when necessary until he could lever her gently to the ground, then he jumped down and landed softly next to her.

'Thank you.' Amy dusted down her skirt and avoided looking at him.

'So. Care to tell me what you were doing up a tree at…' he looked at his watch '…twelve thirty in the morning?'

'What were *you* doing awake?'

'I was up plotting my next attack on the bugs destroying the rose bushes. What do you think? I heard someone screaming like a banshee and thought that I'd better investigate.'

Rafael glanced sideways at the dishevelled figure next to him. He felt utterly bemused by her random behaviour. Like most men, he had certain preferences when it came to women, and was accustomed to certain codes of behaviour. Not even by the wildest stretch of imagination did climbing trees at midnight fit the bill. He tried to picture any one of his erudite, contained and eminently respectable girlfriends up a tree and failed.

'You haven't answered my question and, considering you've put me through a lot of unnecessary hassle, I think I'm owed an explanation. What the hell did you think you were doing?'

Amy gave him her best look of defiance and folded her arms, but he wasn't buying it and eventually she shrugged and looked away. 'Oh, the usual.'

'Which would be…?'

'Girl meets boy, girl likes boy, girl…' she glanced down at her now dirty, creased skirt '…dons new outfit to impress boy only to find that boy has scuttled off to the woods so that he can be with another girl.'

'And in frustration you decided to climb a tree…'

Amy remembered just how obnoxious the man was. She glared at him and told him, sounding to even her own ears like a broken record, to point her in the right direction. At this rate, the infernal man would start thinking that she was stalking him.

'The house is a stiff walk away, at least if you take the direct route, and I certainly won't be sending you back through the deep, dark woods. God knows where you might end up.'

He turned on his heel and started walking away and, with a mixture of frustration and resentment, Amy half ran behind him, struggling to keep up with his long strides.

'I think I can manage!'

Was it possible to read someone's expression from the inclination of their fast-disappearing back? She thought so!

'Please wait!' she yelled. 'These sandals weren't designed for sprinting!'

Rafael stopped and turned around, waiting for her to catch up with him. The woman was truly off her rocker. How many sane human beings climbed trees at midnight in an attempt to deal with a broken heart? In fact, how many sane adults *climbed trees*? He hadn't climbed a tree since he was a kid!

'You should have thought of that before you decided to hike your way across the estate,' Rafael pointed out in the sort of calm voice that someone might use when dealing with the village idiot.

'I wasn't "hiking" my way across the estate,' Amy said icily, 'I was…'

'I'm all ears.' He carried on walking, thankfully at a less ridiculous pace, and she reluctantly fell into step with him.

'Taking a bit of time out to get a breath of fresh air.'

'You seem to do quite a bit of that, don't you? Breathing in the fresh air and covering great distances in the process?'

'Yes, I like walking!'

They had reached his house. Actually just a few more minutes of running would have seen her safely to his front door instead of up a tree, not that *that* option was particularly appealing either, but at least her expensive skirt would still have been intact. Now it was fit only to join the beaded silver shoes in that great wardrobe in the sky.

'You'll have to get out of those things. You're filthy.'

'I want to go back to the house. I *have* to go back there. My clothes are all there.'

'I'm not taking you. You've put me out already.'

'I know it's quite a walk, but you can drive me there, can't you? I mean, you *must* have a car tucked away somewhere.' Amy suddenly felt close to breaking-point. She wrapped her arms tightly around her body and kept herself very still so that she didn't burst into tears.

'I'll run you a bath.'

'Please take me back to the house. Please.'

'You're in no fit state,' Rafael told her without preamble. 'Never mind the state of your clothes, you look as though you're about to collapse. You need to get yourself together. Now sit down. I'll run you a bath and, while it's running, I'll make you something hot to drink.'

The woman was a nuisance but Rafael felt a twinge of concern if only because the same tiring feistiness that got on his nerves was so obviously missing in action.

Before she could launch into another round of pleading to be taken back to the house, he was heading up the stairs so that he could run her a bath. Then he fetched a clean towel from the cupboard and one of his shirts, which she would have to wear whether she liked it or not. He would stick her clothes in the wash and they would be clean in time for her in the morning. After that, he would send her on her way so that she could, presumably, continue to ruin her life by falling in love with inappropriate men.

He returned to find her slumped on the ground in the sitting room.

'I didn't want to get your nice clean furniture dirty,' she said, meeting his questioning eyes. 'I'm disgusting.' She stood up. 'I give you yet another pair of ruined shoes. Two in one day. A record even for me,' she told him gloomily, dangling her sorry sandals in one hand.

'What happened to pair one?' Rafael found himself asking.

'Waterlogged in a kayaking incident this morning.'

'Right. What else? The bathroom is upstairs. Leave your clothes outside the door and I'll stick them in the wash. They'll be ready by morning.'

'I can't spend the night here.' She hovered, tapping one bare foot behind her.

'Have a bath. We'll discuss it when you come out. I've left one of my shirts for you to put on.'

Well, there was nothing to discuss. Amy emerged twenty minutes later, feeling refreshed and wearing only her underwear and his white shirt, which reached a respectable mid-thigh level. It might seem odd to whoever happened to still be up that she was returning to the house in a man's shirt and not much else, but with any luck the place would be dead. Probably aside from James, who would still be gambolling somewhere in the woods with his lady friend. She felt another attack of self-pity threaten and willed it away.

Rafael, looking disgustingly bright-eyed and bushy-tailed, was waiting for her in the sitting room with a cup of hot chocolate on the table, which he pointed at as soon as he saw her.

His shirt drowned her and she was slight enough to begin with. She had scrubbed off all the warpaint and her skin was satin-smooth with a faint golden tan that must have accumulated over the summer. Her eyebrows, in contrast to the vanilla-coloured, unruly hair, were dark. He wondered whether it was this unlikely contrast that lent her face such animation, even when she wasn't speaking. Such as now.

'Feel better?'

'Not much. Thanks for asking.' Amy curled her legs under her and reached forward for the mug, enjoying the creaminess of the drink. She hadn't had hot chocolate for ages. It reminded her of her childhood.

Rafael frowned, a little disconcerted by the bluntness of the reply to a perfectly polite question.

'Your clothes are in the wash,' he informed her, skirting around his reluctant curiosity. 'So, I suppose I *could* drive you back but the car is parked a walk away.'

'Why?'

'Why what?'

'Why is your car parked a walk away? Don't your employers think that you might want to go out now and again? You might be a very diligent gardener, but don't they think that you might want a bit of time out now occasionally?'

'Easier to park it behind the copse on the lane out of the grounds. The alternative would be to drive over the lawns or, of course, through the trees. The grounds were designed with aesthetics in mind and, believe it or not, a strip of tarmac winding across the manicured gardens wasn't considered particularly fetching.'

'Do you *ever* stop being sarcastic?' She sniffed, aware that her composure was very fragile and the gardener was not the sort to make a sympathetic listener.

Amy looked at him. He was leaning forwards, elbows on knees, his hands dangling lightly between his legs. For someone who had been unexpectedly dragged out of a deep sleep, he seemed very well dressed, in a pair of khaki shorts and a short-sleeved shirt, with some worn tan loafers.

'You weren't sleeping, were you?' she asked, to distract herself from thinking about her reasons for being in his house. 'I didn't drag you out of bed with my yelling, did I? You don't look like someone who's been interrupted in the middle of a deep sleep.'

'I was…working, as a matter of fact…'

'You were *working*?' She grinned, forgetting the trauma of her evening for a few minutes. She noticed the sprinkling of dark hair visible just where his collar was open and hurriedly averted her eyes. She wasn't sure why exactly she was aware of the man, but she was. She put it down to his bare-faced arrogance, which would get under anyone's skin. 'Working on what?' she asked, still grinning. 'No, don't tell me…that plot of yours to get rid of the bugs in the rose bushes! Why did you tell me that I'd woken you up? Did you want to make me feel even more guilty than I already felt?'

'There are two bedrooms but one's not made up. I'll take that one and you can have my bed.'

'No way. I'm not sleeping in your bed!'

'Why not?' Rafael asked wearily. 'Come on. Drink that up and go upstairs.'

Amy flushed. He had used that tone of voice with her before. In fact, he seemed to have made a habit of using it since she had made his unfortunate acquaintance. It was the tone of voice of an adult addressing a child. Was that, she wondered, what he thought of her? A kid who got into scrapes?

More to the point, was that, she wondered miserably, what James had thought of her? No more than a kid he could have a joke with?

She quietly placed the mug on the table and stood up, not looking at him, waiting for him to lead her up the stairs, acutely aware that she talked too much, asked too many questions, laughed too loudly. This man might be arrogant and standoffish, but she was in his territory and if he wanted her to shut up, then she would shut up.

Had James wanted her to shut up now and again as well? She had thought he was interested in her but had he been or had he really only been responding to her chattiness, rolling his eyes to the ceiling the minute her back had been turned?

'Okay. Spit it out.'

Amy, staring down as she followed him to the bedroom, almost collided into his huge, immovable frame where he had stopped outside the bedroom door.

'Spit what out?'

'Whatever's eating you up. We might as well forget about getting any sleep tonight.'

Rafael leaned against the doorframe and stared down at her. And this, he thought, was precisely why he didn't go for the emotional types. They poured their hearts out, they sobbed, they *lacked restraint.*

Amy's blue eyes tangled with his deep, deep, almost black ones and she felt momentarily giddy.

'I need to sit down,' she said shakily.

Rafael stood aside and made a sweeping gesture in the direction of his bed, which, to Amy, looked unbelievably tempting. To hell with prudish, maidenly qualms. She was suddenly exhausted.

His bed smelt of *him,* a clean, masculine smell that made her want to close her eyes and inhale deeply because it was a weirdly *comforting* smell. And why pretend? She had grown up bunking down and sharing beds. Her mother had sworn that it did the immune system a world of good. She slipped under the luxurious, silky soft quilt and yawned.

'I just can't believe it,' Amy said, just as Rafael was about to leave the room and head back downstairs so that he could resume the conference call to Australia that had been so rudely interrupted. He turned around and narrowed his eyes on the small figure now propped up against the pillows. She looked ridiculously fragile, he thought, which seemed incongruous considering the size of her mouth.

'Can't believe what?' Rafael was not a man who was accustomed to the emotional complexities of women. He had always listened to James's tales of woe with a certain amount of amusement and privately congratulated himself on his wisdom in going for women who didn't play games or have moods or weren't, in short, a mess. He didn't sleep around and his breakups had never been messy. At thirty-four, which didn't exactly qualify him as The Old Man of the Sea, he nevertheless considered himself pretty much together emotionally. A man who knew what he wanted in life, and that included women.

'Can't believe how I could ever have been *so stupid.* I mean…' Amy's voice wobbled as she considered the depth of her stupidity '…just because he looked at me once or twice and chatted now and again…how could I have got it into my head? I mean…has that ever happened to you? Has it? You just completely misread someone else's signals and then fabricate a whole fairy tale in your head that's just way, *way* off target?'

'No.'

'What…*never?*' Amy asked, temporarily disconcerted.

'Never.'

'Oh. So I guess you wouldn't really know what it's like to be…to be…'

'No. I wouldn't.' He was fairly sure he was about to find out, unless, of course, he put a stop to this nonsense, shut the bedroom door firmly and only resurfaced when she was about to leave in the morning. 'But I can tell you that he's not worth it.'

Amy tried to focus on James, his charming, boyish face, his blond hair that always managed to look ever so slightly tousled, though out of the corner of her eye she couldn't help but notice Rafael's brooding presence by the door. He was probably sick to death of her, she couldn't help thinking, but for some reason she didn't want to be on her own. She felt too vulnerable.

'You can't say that. You don't know him.'

'I know that no one is worth shedding tears over.'

'Oh!' Reluctantly she abandoned the temptation to wallow and frowned at Rafael curiously. 'I guess you've never been in love…'

Rafael was fast regretting his impulse to listen to the woman because he had momentarily felt sorry for her.

'I'm not entirely sure I believe in the concept,' he told her abruptly. 'Romantics hang onto the idea for dear life because they think it makes sense of life, but for me…no. I think I'll avoid it like the plague if the net result is what I'm looking at right now.'

Amy got up the energy to glare but it didn't last long. 'At least we Romantics have fun!'

'If fun is lying on a stranger's bed at one-thirty in the morning blubbing…' Rafael said dryly and Amy was forced to concede defeat.

'Okay. You win. I'm a fool. Maybe next time lucky.' She gave him a watery grin and it was such a brave pretence of a smile that Rafael found himself reluctantly smiling back. 'Maybe,' she mused, 'next time I won't fall for the boss…'

CHAPTER THREE

OKAY. Rafael was man enough to admit it to himself the following morning. He was curious. He could only assume that that was what enforced solitude did to a person, because his contact with the outside world, for the past three days, had been limited to telephone conversations or, more often than not, communication via e-mail.

At the time, he had not envisaged this as a problem. Work could be done as easily via computers and fax machines as it could be done face to face and he had made damned sure that he had total access to the outside world thanks to the telephone people who had installed everything he could possibly need for speedy connection to the Internet. At the click of a button he had been able to give his secretary all the instructions she needed to ensure that the numerous tentacles of his highly profitable companies were operating perfectly.

He had even, in the deepest corners of his mind, used the uninvited situation to his own advantage.

He paused for a few seconds, frowning into the distance as he thought about Elizabeth, the eminently suitable Elizabeth, and their very civilised parting. One that he had instigated although, when he thought about it logically, he couldn't quite understand what had prompted his decision because she was everything he wanted, at least on paper.

He had met her when she had been heading the team of lawyers they had used eight months previously to sort out some complex legal problems on a takeover he had been finalising. He had been impressed, first, by her immense competence and her cool, self-assured manner. Later, by the many things they had in common, ranging from opera to theatre, from jazz music to fine wines.

And to complete the perfect picture, she was just the sort of leggy brunette he favoured, with short, tailored hair and an elegant appreciation of everything cultured.

It had been a little unnerving that his mother had taken an instant dislike to the woman, but Rafael had not allowed that to trouble the very real ideas he had been nurturing about taking the inevitable plunge into matrimony. As arrangements went, it would have been perfect simply because they were so alike in so many ways.

He wasn't quite sure when doubts had set in, but eventually the very perfect nature of their relationship had started to feel just a little dull. Three weeks ago he had been visited by an unsettling vision of Elizabeth and himself twenty years down the road, an elegant but essentially boring middle-aged couple still frequenting the opera, having raised their very perfect but essentially boring children to do exactly the same.

He had withdrawn from the relationship and finally broken it off knowing that ten days in the Hamptons, away from any company dos that they might mutually attend, would be beneficial for both of them.

Which brought him back to his curiosity about the creature still lying upstairs in his bed, having fallen asleep on him just when she had revealed the object of her unrequited passion.

He filled a mug with steaming fresh coffee and headed up

the stairs, pausing in the doorway to his bedroom so that he could look, dispassionately, at the woman lying on his bed.

Everything about her was in a state of disarray. Her blonde hair was all over the place, the covers had obviously been tossed aside then yanked back on several times during the course of the past few hours and were now half off the bed. One very slim foot hung over one side, affording him the sight of toenails painted a very unconservative shade of purple. Her hands were flung out over her head. A trusting person, he thought absent-mindedly, hence the way she was sleeping on her back. No wonder James had been able to hook her without trying.

'Time to get up, Sleeping Beauty.' He strolled over to the curtains and yanked them open so that Amy sat up with an indignant cry, shielding her eyes from the sudden, horrible, intrusive glare.

'I've brought you up some coffee.' No, he was not going to get into any heart-to-heart conversations about what had happened the night before. He didn't want to invite any confidences. Never mind the curiosity. 'And your clothes are all laundered.'

'There was no need for you to pull open the curtains like that!' Amy groaned, subsiding back onto the bed and stuffing a pillow over her face.

Rafael calmly walked towards her and jerked the pillow away, holding it out of reach while she tried to scrabble uselessly for it, finally giving up and propping herself up on the palms of her hands, all the better to deliver her best glare.

'What time is it?' she asked, shoving herself further up the bed and helping herself to the extremely welcome mug of coffee that he had placed on the table next to her. She groaned louder when he told her and reached for her mobile phone. Naturally it wasn't there as she had left the party the night before and headed to shores unknown without thinking that she might finish up the evening up a tree. She would have to say that the Girl Guide organisation did not prepare you for *every eventuality* despite what they might like to promise!

'Oh, God.' She looked at him despairingly. 'What's Claire going to be thinking?'

'Who's Claire?'

'Not to mention everyone else! I was supposed to be on the beach, picnic, barbecue thing with them today… I even brought a special outfit…' She gritted her teeth in frustration and looked at Rafael accusingly. It was all right for him to stand there, all fresh as a daisy, with only lawnmowers and gardens on his mind, while she was in a state of emotional agony!

'No need to worry. I phoned the house.'

'You did *what*?'

'Phoned the house.' Rafael raised his eyebrows in a question. 'What's the problem?'

'*What's the problem?*' Amy digested the image of her best friend chortling at her high jinks with all their friends. 'What did you say?' she asked, with less panic in her voice, hoping that he had not seen fit to share each and every detail of the sorry situation that had landed her sleeping in his bed.

'I said you went out to get some air, lost your way and by the time you showed up at my front door it was too late to send you back and you were exhausted. So I very kindly allowed you to stay the night and would be sending you back to base first thing. Does that meet with your approval?'

'I can see it doesn't meet with *yours,* judging from that tone of voice.'

'Are you forgetting that you should be grateful to me for getting you out of that tree…?' He watched as her face blanched.

'Who did you speak to?'

'Oh, your boss, of course.'

Horrible man, he turned his back on her and was now staring through the window at what promised to be a dream of a day as far as the weather went.

'You spoke to James…'

'Who else?'

'What did you tell him?' Amy asked in a small voice.

'Oh, just that you spent the night roaming the woods with lovelorn heart only to find your beloved in a clinch with another woman, at which point you decided to climb a tree, from whence I was forced to rescue you…'

'You *didn't*!'

'Of course I didn't!' Rafael turned around just in time to catch the pillow that was winging its way in the direction of his head. He patted it back into shape and tossed it on the chair by the window, where it joined all the other assorted bits of paraphernalia that were slowly building up to a veritable mountain of odds and ends.

'Who do you think she was?' Amy mused aloud, resting her face thoughtfully in the palm of her hand and gently tapping her front tooth with one absent-minded finger. 'I mean, she wasn't one of us…'

'Your clothes are downstairs. As is breakfast if you want anything to eat. Then you can be on your way.' Rafael was disconcerted to find his eyes straying to the pointed tips of her breasts nudging the thin fabric of his cotton shirt. He frowned, irritated with himself, and looked at her face. 'So come on. Up.'

'Yes, all right. I won't be in your hair for any longer than is necessary!'

'I'll leave your clothes outside the bedroom door. You can have a shower if you want.' It was already ten in the morning. The woman had wreaked havoc with his working day. He had no intention of prolonging the unwelcome situation. Mind made up, Rafael left her to her own devices, making sure that the clothes were outside the door as promised, just in case she decided to lounge around in his house all day in an attempt to recover from her broken heart, wearing only his shirt. What ever happened to female modesty? He was no prude but he did expect a certain amount of decorum from women. His mind drifted away from the report flickering on the screen in front of him. He imagined her stripping off that shirt in one easy, fluid movement, letting it drop to the floor while she casually walked over it *en route* to the bathroom.

He frowned and pushed the intrusive thoughts out of his mind, focusing one hundred per cent on his work and only looking up when she padded into the room, fully dressed although barefoot.

'What on earth are you doing?' Amy asked, surprised to find him in front of a laptop computer, never mind the complicated rows of numbers he seemed to be staring at.

Rafael quickly snapped it shut. James knew that she had spent the night in the guest house, had chuckled too much for Rafael's liking about it as a matter of fact, but had reluctantly conceded that it would be best all round if she wasn't informed of his real identity.

'She's under the impression that I'm the gardener,' Rafael told his brother and then proceeded to wait while James roared with laughter down the end of the line, prompting Rafael to ask just what was so inconceivable about the misconception.

'The thought of you being happy with mowing lawns,' James finished with a grin in his voice. 'Maybe if you were test-driving the lawnmower you had invented having started up the company that would eventually take over every other lawnmowing business in the universe…'

'You make me sound like a megalomaniac,' Rafael said irritably.

'Well, one of us has to be and it certainly won't be me,' James told him amicably.

'Anyway,' Rafael said, wrapping up the conversation, 'if she knows who I am, then I shall have no choice but to put in an appearance.'

'And I don't need you being a fly in my ointment, big brother, so I'm happy to keep it under wraps. Anyway, she'll do you good.'

'I very much doubt that,' Rafael said curtly. 'The woman has a screw loose.' He had a sudden vision of her clinging onto the branch of the tree for dear life and almost grinned at the thought. 'I don't generally have much interest in madwomen.'

'Right…well…tell her we'll see her later…'

And later, he now thought, couldn't come quickly enough. He looked at her and had to admit to himself that she looked a great deal better in the freshly cleaned clothes and not covered with dirt and grime.

'Well?' Amy prompted, strolling over so that she could position herself behind him and attempt to open up the lid of the computer that he had snapped shut over his shoulder. Rafael gripped both her wrists and tugged her gently so that she very nearly lost her footing and fell against him.

Amy felt her heart stop then quicken until she was feeling a little faint. Something about the broad hardness of his back against her chest and the feel of his fingers circling her wrists…

Having spent a lifetime being totally at ease in the company of the opposite sex, Amy now felt strangely and disconcertingly awkward and exposed as he brought her around to face him, still holding onto her.

'Ever heard of *personal space*?' Rafael asked. Her wrists felt like twigs between his fingers. He had never felt anyone as delicate as her before. He released her and folded his arms behind his head.

'Sorry…I'm just so accustomed…to…' She fell silent and rubbed her wrists, unconsciously taking a couple of steps backwards then laughing at herself for acting like a fool.

'To…?' He stood up and headed towards the kitchen and Amy fell in behind him.

There. It somehow seemed a lot safer talking to a back. 'To a big family. Three brothers.' Amy laughed as she regained her composure, although she was still rubbing her wrists as if trying to disperse the sudden heat she had felt there. 'And a pretty small house. I guess the personal space thing wasn't really in evidence a lot…so…I'm sorry…'

'Apology accepted. Now, what would you like for breakfast?' He pulled open the fridge and Amy's mouth dropped open. She had expected a carton of milk edging towards its sell by date, maybe an egg or two, a few cans of beer and a block of cheese. Instead she was presented with an abundance of edible delights. Smoked salmon shared shelf space with what looked like some pretty expensive pâtè, a dozen eggs were neatly housed above the shelf with some white wine, there was salad, bright green and fresh, and a variety of different cheeses. As a caterer, she was used to rapid visual scans of cupboards and fridges and she had never seen a better, or more expensively stocked one in a very long time.

She reached in and extracted the packet of duck pâtè.

'Help yourself,' Rafael said dryly.

'Fantastic assortment,' Amy breathed. To hell with personal space, she had to have a closer look at the yummy contents of his refrigerator. 'Sorry to be nosy…' She peered in and would have investigated further had he not smartly shut the door on her enquiring face.

'I'll get some bread. Sit down.'

Amy obediently sat at the kitchen table, which was a chrome and granite testimony to expensive modern living. She wondered how a humble gardener, non humble though he might be in character, could afford such luxury and decided that James must foot the bill or, rather, his mother who owned the house.

'Interesting…' She couldn't help herself. She held up the nutty roll and twirled it thoughtfully between her fingers.

'The *roll* is interesting?' Rafael asked, pouring himself another cup of coffee and swinging round one of the chairs so that he could straddle it and face her.

'*Very interesting.*' Amy's voice was loaded with intent. 'Involved in the food business as I am, I would suggest that this is a home-made granary roll, not your average supermarket all-air-and-no-substance look-alike…'

'Where are you going with this?'

'Straight to this question…' She slit it open with her fingers and dived into the most delicious breakfast of pâtè and bread she had had in years. 'How does the gardener afford a fridge full of the finest food money can buy?'

Rafael, having seen fit to economise with the truth when it came to his identity, could now only think on his feet.

'Why not?' He shrugged. 'I'm a man of taste, whatever my profession, and as you can see I have no family on which to spend the money I earn.' That much was true enough at any rate.

'What happens if you *do* decide to…you know…get married, start a family? I mean, I know you said you're no Romantic, but even boring pragmatists eventually meet the right woman and get married… What I'm saying is this… would you have to leave this fantastic place?' She had a dreamy mouthful of pâtè and nutty bread and looked at him as she ate.

He really was striking, in a rough sort of way. Charmless, of course, she told herself, quickly remembering the way he had snapped to her about his 'personal space', as if he believed he had every right to dictate.

'I can't believe the extent of your nosiness,' Rafael said wonderingly. 'Trust me when I tell you this—should you ever grow bored with the catering business, then private investigator would be right up your street.' And what did she mean by boring pragmatist?

'It was just a question,' Amy said, hurt. 'I didn't think I was invading your precious personal space. It's no wonder you can't get soul mate lady gardener to share your life with you! Not if you make a habit of jumping down people's throats the minute they ask you a perfectly normal question!'

'I don't happen to be looking for a soul mate, lady gardener or otherwise,' Rafael grated, thinking of cool, sophisticated, attorney ex-girlfriend Elizabeth. 'And to answer your perfectly normal if incredibly nosey question, yes, the house is mine whatever my personal circumstances.'

'Wow.' Amy finished the last of the roll with some regret.

Which signalled the time for her departure, Rafael thought. And he could get down to some work. He had overslept, a first for him considering he had often worked through the night and had successfully made do with a couple of hours' sleep before facing the day with spring in his step. He could only assume that listening to a ranting emotional female was a hell of a lot more stressful than closing a deal.

'Still…I guess you must find it a bit…difficult in some ways…'

It was like seeing a trap lurking in the distance, knowing that the simple way to sidestep the threat would involve just one simple manoeuvre, and yet pushing on straight into the ambush, eyes wide open. Rafael knew that he should just ignore her loaded, obscure remark and hustle her out of the house and yet…

'I have no idea what you're on about now,' he told her, getting an annoyingly speculative once over for his remark.

'Well…' Amy remembered his 'personal space' remark and realised, before she did her usual and spoke without thinking, that she was on the verge of crashing through his Do Not Enter sign with a resounding bang. She stood up, glanced around for her ruined sandals, which seemed to have been put through a wash cycle and now appeared unwearable, and walked towards the door.

'Doesn't matter,' she threw over her shoulder. 'I'm going to go now and leave you in peace, if you don't mind pointing me in the right direction. I think I can manage the walk back now!'

'You're too late to catch any of the day trips,' Rafael told her. For some reason it irritated him that she hadn't finished what she had been intending to say. What was even more irritating was the fact that she had not been trying out the coy ploy by leaving him hanging on. No, he got the feeling that she had, at the last minute, reconsidered voicing her thoughts because *she felt sorry for him*. In the great scheme of things, no one felt sorry for Rafael Vives. At least not the Rafael Vives who inhabited the rarefied world of the extremely wealthy, the extremely powerful and hence the extremely respected.

'I know.' She was inspecting her sandals as if hoping that they might reveal themselves as wearable after all. But no. The dainty straps, like strings of cleverly positioned tan spaghetti, were mangled beyond redemption. She picked them up with a little sigh of resignation and looked at Rafael. 'Everyone will have left at nine-thirty. Walking along the golden sands, having a fun barbecue on the beach…well, who needs that when you can slink back to an empty house and spend the day on your own by a deserted pool?' Amy said mournfully.

'I don't think you'll be slinking anywhere on those shoes,' Rafael said, his lips twitching. 'I'm afraid I slung them in with the clothes thinking it would do the trick.'

'That would have worked if they'd been made out of

cloth,' Amy told him, with a reluctant grin. 'Don't worry. They were useless anyway. James didn't look at me twice when I had them on.'

Rafael made his mind up. To hell with the work. It would keep. 'Come on. We'll take the car.'

Amy wasn't about to look a gift horse in the mouth. She accepted the ride with alacrity.

What was less easy to swallow was the car waiting for them when they finally hit the path that circled the vast grounds. No muddy four wheel drive. Instead a low-slung sports car, Rafael's own tribute to a recklessness that his very controlled and highly organised life lacked.

'Don't say a word,' he warned her, beeping it open from the key ring in his trouser pocket.

'Wouldn't dream of it.' She allowed him to open her door for her, appreciating the display of good manners, which she wasn't accustomed to seeing, and slid in. Inside was as gleaming as outside, from the spotless cream leather bucket seats to the walnut dashboard in which she could see her reflection if she peered hard enough. She turned to him with a grin and couldn't resist adding, 'Although I'd love to be a fly on the wall when you *do* meet that soul mate gardener of yours, the one you say you're not looking for!'

'I won't even bother to ask you what you're on about because I know you're going to tell me anyway.' He felt a sudden rush of carefree abandon as his car roared into life and he began eating up the perimeter road, heading out of the estate towards…the town centre? One of the beaches?

Amy, giving him her undivided attention, was blissfully unaware that he was driving away from the direction of the house. In fact, she was blissfully unaware of pretty much everything aside from his strong, determined profile, the slight smile tugging the corners of his mouth, the hand resting lightly on the steering wheel, a man in complete charge of his machine.

'Well, if you insist on knowing, and please don't give me a long, boring sermon on infringing your personal space when you've given me permission to tell you what I'm thinking…'

Rafael flicked her a wry, sidelong glance.

'…but I'd love to see you when the time comes for you to part with this sports car…boys and their toys…'

'I'm not following you.'

'Well, you can afford all this stuff now because you have no responsibilities…aside from the gardens, of course,' she added hastily, because it infuriated her when other people downgraded her own job just because it didn't involve wearing a suit or working in front of a computer, 'but believe me this will be the first thing you'll have to jettison when you get a wife and start having a family.' She sneaked a look at him and something peculiar happened in her stomach when she imagined what his kids would look like. She looked away hurriedly.

'Just another reason why I'm not on the lookout for the soul mate.' Rafael grinned and looked across at her. 'And by the way, we're not heading back to the house just yet…'

'We're not? Why not?' She felt something akin to a prickle of excitement and explained it away as sheer relief that she would be spared having to spend the whole day on her own, moping about James.

'I feel morally obliged to replace the shoes I destroyed,' Rafael told her gravely so that Amy didn't know whether he was being serious or not.

'There's no need,' Amy told him quickly. 'Honestly. I have my trainers and I can always borrow some of Claire's shoes. We're the same size.'

'I wouldn't hear of it.'

'But what about your work? You were busy on the

computer this morning. I wouldn't want to interrupt…whatever it was you were doing…'

'Now why do I get the feeling that there's an undercurrent of sarcasm there?'

'You're not much like a gardener, are you?' Amy teased, enjoying the moment.

'I don't know. Have you met a lot of gardeners?'

'I've met a lot of…all types.' Amy laughed.

'You should be careful when you say things like that,' Rafael said, flicking a glance in her direction. 'Men might get the wrong impression.'

'Well, they'd be wrong,' Amy told him truthfully. She turned away and stared out of the window. While she had been engaged in conversation, the stunning scenery had been flashing past her. Now she took her time to drink it in and Rafael swiftly changed the subject. He really had no idea how their conversation had moved so quickly into personal territory, nor did he know why the hell he had made the decision to drive her into the town to get a pair of shoes. Since when did he ever go shopping with a woman? It simply was one of those pastimes he preferred to avoid. He knew nothing about choosing women's clothing and cared even less. He had always found James's interest in shopping, be it for himself or whatever woman he happened to be with, very amusing.

So why, he asked himself now, the unnecessary trip? He frowned and pushed the uninvited question out of his head. There was a lot to tell her about Long Island and he did. The beaches were spectacular, as were the pine forests with their quiet nature trails and the secluded freshwater ponds. What he had no need to mention, but what Amy saw perfectly well for herself, was that the place reeked of money. She had no idea how much a simple pair of sandals was going to cost, but she was pretty sure it would be beyond her modest budget and she awkwardly explained that to Rafael when they had eventually arrived at the quaint, perfectly preserved little town with its frighteningly expensive-looking boutiques.

'I'll take care of it,' Rafael said, neatly parking the car and turning to look at her before he opened his door.

'You can't "take care of it". And anyway, why should you?'

'I washed the damn things.'

'Which you had to do because I tramped miles across the estate and landed up in a tree.'

'At least you seem to have cured yourself of your broken heart,' Rafael told her, swinging away and letting himself out of the car before she had a chance to reply. 'I thought,' he carried on, leaning on the bonnet of the car as he waited for her to emerge, 'I might have been dealing with a sobbing mess, but if all your emotions are focused on whether I should or shouldn't pay for a pair of shoes for you, then it's fair to say that you're over your boss. Love is cheap, isn't it?' He raised one amused eyebrow and she could have belted him.

'I…I…just didn't want to bore you with my emotions!' Amy spluttered. She'd spent many months cheerfully infatuated with James. There was no way she was going to be accused of being shallow, of *getting over it all* in a matter of seconds.

'Oh. I suppose I should be grateful for that in that case.' He slammed shut his car door and waited until she was standing by his side, barely reaching his shoulder with her high-heeled sandals off. He looked down at her bare feet. 'We'd better get you some shoes quickly.' Which brought her full circle, back to the distraction of trying to persuade him that there was no need to fork out—*how much?*—for a pair of shoes. Not when he was just a lowly worker like herself and she knew how much the passing overpriced purchase could hurt…even when the shoes in question were undeniably…she twirled one slender foot with appreciation…

gorgeous. Flat, tanned and perfectly functional were it not for the tiny exotic row of diamond look-alikes across the straps. They would look perfect with trousers or a skirt and absolutely radiated femininity.

Rafael looked on as she tested them in the shop, pausing in front of the mirror for further, more detailed inspection. Unlike James, he was a mind man, a guy who liked what happened in a woman's head rather than what took place on the outside, although it had to be said that he had thus far never had a problem finding women who were a happy mixture of both. This woman, whatever the hell happened or didn't happen in her head, was the epitome of femininity, he conceded, from the blonde cloud of hair to the dainty ankles that were now being paraded in front of him for his inspection. He grunted.

'I can't get them unless we go halves,' Amy said firmly. 'They're just way too expensive.' Staring down at her feet, she missed the puzzled look Rafael received from the boutique owner and the quick shake of his head in response.

He shrugged and agreed. Had she but known the vast extent of his personal fortune, he wondered whether she would have been quite so considerate of his finances. He also wondered whether James's bank balance had played any role in her infatuation. She gave the impression of being utterly transparent, but serious wealth was a harsh teacher when it came to matters of trust.

It was perfectly clear to him that what she felt for his stepbrother was simply a mild case of infatuation and there was no chance that James would fall for her charms, at least not the James that he knew, but just in case Rafael decided that it was his duty to ensure that the unthinkable didn't happen. He didn't know the first thing about the woman but certainly her profession predisposed him to think that the lure of someone else's money might be very strong indeed.

'Oh, for goodness' sake!' Amy hissed to him under her breath. 'There's no need to look so grumpy!'

'Do you always have to say exactly what's on your mind the minute the thought occurs?'

'If by that you mean am I a pretty honest person, then yes!'

'Are you now?' He handed over his credit card but continued to look at her so thoughtfully that Amy eventually released one long, laborious sigh.

'Yes. Yes, I try to be.'

Rafael decided that he would come to that later. He handed over the bag with the shoes, which she immediately put on with a smile.

'You like pretty things, don't you?' he mused, knowing that that in itself might well be a mark against her, but still reluctantly enjoying her obvious delight in her purchase. She was like a kid with a new toy. Having never indulged in shopping expeditions with women, he wondered whether Elizabeth would have taken similar pleasure in the purchase of a new pair of shoes, and reckoned not. For starters she wasn't a strappy, diamante-beaded sandal kind of woman and he doubted a pair of high black shoes would arouse a similar enthusiasm.

'Show me a woman who doesn't,' Amy quipped, looking up at him and grinning, even though he still looked as sombre as a judge, 'and I'll show you a liar.'

It was virtually impossible not to smile back at her.

'Let's get some lunch.'

'Okay, but I have an idea. Let's grab some swimsuits and head for the beach with a picnic.' Everyone else would be doing it. Maybe on another of the beaches, but still out in the glorious sunshine, having fun, swimming. She mournfully thought how far she had travelled in the space of a few short hours. From looking forward to wearing her little turquoise bikini in an attempt to show James that she was more than just a convenient caterer, she was now making do with a perfect stranger who made no bones about letting her know that she was, by and large, a nuisance, someone who looked as though a foul temper was just part and parcel of his personality, just the sort of person she would, by nature, avoid at all costs, in fact!

She almost expected him to shoot her idea dead in the water, but to her surprise he agreed without hesitation.

'A long lazy lunch on a beach somewhere,' Rafael murmured, 'sounds like a very good idea to me…' And a very effective way of finding out just what you're all about…

CHAPTER FOUR

IMPULSIVE by nature, Amy was accustomed to deciding on a course of action only to belatedly consider the drawbacks. A spontaneous picnic on a beach would have meant time wasted wondering what swimsuit to wear, what clothes to take to the beach, what food to buy and how to transport it. She was unprepared for the stunning efficiency with which Rafael proceeded. He gave her five minutes to fly inside the house and get whatever gear she needed, including, he told her, ample sunblock because he had no intention of driving her to the nearest emergency ward should she get sunburn.

'Oh, charming,' Amy muttered, but she did exactly as he had ordered. From there, the entire trip seemed to be wrapped up in under five seconds. He left the engine running while he sprinted to his house, returning in the requisite five minutes wearing swimming trunks, a baggy tee shirt and a towel slung over one shoulder. And sunglasses. Dark sunglasses that brought out his Mediterranean heritage.

Then onto a gorgeous little deli. She would have liked to have gone along with him and enjoyed a good, long browse at the exciting array of food, but, as if reading her mind, he told her to wait in the car for him. Typical caveman, she thought disgruntledly, probably a legacy of that macho heritage of his. It didn't escape her notice that a fair number of women seemed to quite like that caveman look!

Amy pointedly looked away as he slipped into the seat next to her and said that all that was left now was to hit the beach. And there were a lot to choose from, depending on how long they wanted to spend in the car.

'I don't mind the drive,' he murmured in a voice that told her that he was laughing at her. 'Might just as well make use of the sports car before I have to sell it to support the wife and kids.'

'Glad you're coming around to my point of view,' Amy said loftily, refusing to be needled into a response. But she *did* feel needled, and not by anything he said but by the way he *looked*. It was ridiculous, crazy. The man wasn't her type. The macho types had never held much appeal for her, too much in the muscle department and too little in the sense-of-humour department, and, above all else, Amy liked a guy with a sense of humour.

But some of the things the gardener said… She stole a quick glance at the strong profile with just the ghost of a smile playing on his lips and blinked in confusion.

'Guess you probably have the same problem as well…'

'What problem would that be?'

'Knowing that your luxuries in life will have to go when you get married and give up work…'

Amy burst out laughing. 'First of all, I don't intend to "give up work" the minute I get married! Sure, I might use it as an opportunity to break out on my own instead of working for a company, but that would depend on who I marry, wouldn't it? And secondly, I don't have any luxuries along the lines that you're thinking! Not all of us are lucky enough to have a grace and favour residence at our disposal!' Enraptured by the sight of sand dunes rolling down to the ocean, Amy embarked on a series of excitable questions, but Rafael was having none of that. For the moment, his tour guide hat was going to remain off.

He pulled up to the beach, to which he seemed to have automatic resident's access, and watched her run ahead of him, kicking the sand between her toes. She had changed into a pair of faded denim cut-offs and a thin white tee shirt, which she proceeded to take off while on the move, revealing a small turquoise bikini top. An extremely small turquoise bikini top. Rafael drew his breath in sharply. From the looks of it, she certainly had come equipped to knock the socks off James. He wondered what else was in her wardrobe and the speed with which his mind filled the gaps brought a dull colour to his cheeks. He frowned, irritated with himself for being sidetracked, but then he had been irritated with himself since his decision to abandon his laptop this morning.

All for a good cause! he reminded himself.

She was racing back towards him now, breathless with apology for not helping carry some of the picnic. Behind his sunglasses, Rafael's eyes drifted to the pert breasts barely covered by her top, and to the washboard-flat stomach. She had a slender graceful figure with small breasts and he found the flair of her hips from her tiny waist mesmerizing.

Feeling a treacherous sense of arousal, Rafael quickened his pace.

'Fine, Mr He-Man! It's absolutely all right by me if you want to prove how big and strong you are!' Except he *was* big and strong. Very big. Amy paused and then continued in his wake.

He had thought to bring a rug, something he kept in the boot of his car, as did most people who lived in any place where white-out conditions could occur in winter. He laid this out now, dumped the bags of food on it and waited for her to join him.

'Short legs,' Amy told him. 'Not good in sand.' She looked out to the sea, anywhere but into those disconcerting dark shades. 'Fantastic. I haven't been to many beaches in my life, but this is one of the best.' They were both standing and she was beginning to feel a little ridiculous and very conscious of her sparingly cut bikini top. It would never have stood out in a group of people, with the girls sporting similar beachwear, but in front of Rafael she suddenly felt *exposed*. She promptly spread out her towel and sat on it, relaxing back on her elbows.

To her relief he did likewise, and she had to admit as he stripped off his shirt that gardening had certainly worked for him when it came to endowing him with a pretty impressive physique. There was not an ounce of spare flesh on the man and with every small movement she could see the definition of sinew and muscle. She felt her mouth go dry.

Surely he hadn't been right when he had implied that she was shallow? That she had shrugged off the small matter of a broken heart in record time because she was some kind of airhead who fell in and out of love for fun?

'I wonder where they've all gone…' Amy mused aloud, thinking that she might just steer the conversation onto James and try and emerge in a positive light, because it was fast occurring to her that what she had felt for James had been nothing more lasting, she was ashamed to admit, than a summer cold.

'Why?' Rafael said bluntly. 'Your mission no longer is to try and charm your boss into the sack. Unless, of course, you've already jumped into bed with him and this is just a consolidation exercise…?'

Amy shot up and twisted round to look at him, her cheeks red with outrage.

'How dare you?' She jumped to her feet and began striding off. When she felt his hand bear down on her arm, she didn't bother to look around. She just attempted to shrug him off, but it was like trying to shrug off a ring of steel and in the end she was forced to turn around.

'You make a habit of this, don't you? Is that how you

deal with tricky conversations? Or tricky situations? By walking off as fast as you can in whatever direction your feet might take you?'

Having twice landed on his doorstep for that very reason, Amy struggled to come up with a snappy riposte. 'Do you mind? You're hurting me!' It was the best she could do and he released her immediately. She could see him visibly regain his composure. 'I don't intend to sit on a beach with you and eat...bloody sandwiches on the sand while you insult me!' She took a couple of steps back and glared at him. 'You owe me an *apology*!'

'I beg your pardon?' In his entire life, no one had ever demanded an apology from Rafael. He was, literally, astounded by the request.

'You heard me, buster! I want an apology from you! You just insulted me, in case you'd forgotten!'

'I did not insult you.'

'You accused me of being the sort of girl who sleeps around.'

'I made an educated guess.'

'Well, it was the *wrong* educated guess and I'm not budging from here until you apologise!' Amy didn't know why on earth she was getting so steamed up. *She* knew the truth and wasn't that all that mattered? But she could feel her eyes pricking from the effort of holding back a sudden onset of tears. She had a sudden vision of James with his mystery woman and was overcome by a sense of pathos.

'Oh, for God's sake,' Rafael muttered stiffly. 'I apologise if you found my remark offensive.'

'Good—' Amy sniffed '—because I did.'

'I really don't know what you see in him,' Rafael said, once they were back on the rug with a state of temporary truce between them. Amy had made her mind up that she wasn't going to let the man get under her skin. She would never be in this part of the world again and she was determined to enjoy the experience. She gave Rafael a withering glance.

'Would that be because you *know him so well*?' she asked scathingly. 'I know he's your boss, but he spends all his time in London. In fact, I bet he's hardly out here at all! When he comes to America, he probably heads straight for the New York office!'

Rafael stifled a grin. Whenever James came to America, the first place he visited was their mother's house in the Hamptons. The office was just that glass building he popped into to show his face.

'He occasionally comes out to the house,' Rafael said diplomatically. He lay flat on the rug, hands behind his head, the dark shades protecting his eyes from the glare of the sun. He felt pleasurably relaxed and realised that it was the first time in years that he had *done nothing*. It seemed ironic that it would be in the company of a woman who rubbed every nerve in his body the wrong way. But still... He watched as the sun forced her out of her cut offs, revealing a neat, but perfectly proportioned body. And the bikini bottom was just as skimpy as the top.

'Oh, and from the occasional visit, you think you know him?'

'You think *you* do?' Rafael turned the question over to her. He had the whole day and he intended to use it to his advantage. He would find out just what her intentions were and he foresaw no problem in unearthing the information. The woman was hardly backward at coming forward, and, anyway, he was an expert when it came to extracting what he wanted.

'Of course I do!' Amy snapped, rolling over onto her side and propping herself up so that she could direct the full force of her scowl at Rafael's harshly beautiful profile. 'Not that it's any of your business!' She fulminated silently as he continued to stare upwards, apparently oblivious to her presence.

'He's very funny and incredibly popular. In fact, I don't think there's anyone who doesn't fall for James's charm!'

'And how often did you actually get to talk to him?' Rafael asked curiously.

'We joked around. I handle all of the catering for the directors. Most of the time it's just a case of deliver, but ever, so often James would commission me to do something special for friends. Actually, I've even been to his place to do private functions.'

'So he's friendly towards you and, on the back of that, you decide that you'll fall in love.'

Amy felt herself rush towards anger, then she considered what he had said, the starkly ridiculous thumbnail image he had presented, and sighed. 'He caught me when I was vulnerable,' she admitted. There was something solidly reassuring about the brute lying on the rug next to her. Sensitive he most certainly was not, but his unadorned honesty didn't seem like such a bad thing just at the moment.

'Vulnerable…from what?'

'How are you when it comes to listening?' Amy asked, resuming her horizontal position on the rug, so that they were both now staring towards the heavens, Amy with her eyes closed.

Rafael, with his line of perfectly groomed, perfectly controlled, high-powered ex-girlfriends, wondered what exactly *listening* entailed when asked by the woman lying next to him.

'Inexperienced,' he said deflatingly, although he was aware that he was being gifted a golden opportunity to find out what, if any, were her intentions towards his brother.

'Really?' Amy was distracted. He seemed to have that effect on her, she had noticed. One minute she would be going along just fine, and then the next minute he had managed to swing her off onto a tangent until she forgot what she had been talking about in the first place. 'Is that because you don't have many opportunities to…meet women?' The thought seemed ludicrous now that she had voiced it. Women had stared at him wherever they went. She had noticed it. Sidelong, interested glances. She was pretty sure that the man could get a woman if he only emerged once a year from that house of his under cover of darkness. 'No, forget I said that. You meet lots of women; you just don't much care what's going on in their heads.'

Rafael flushed darkly. 'I meet lots of women who don't see it as their duty to keep me advised of their every thought on a minute-by-minute basis,' he corrected through gritted teeth.

'Okay.' Amy wondered what sort of women such a species would be.

'But,' Rafael said heavily, 'we were talking about you. You said that you were…vulnerable.'

The word 'vulnerable' emerged from his mouth as though being aired for the very first time. It made Amy want to laugh.

'I'd just broken up with my boyfriend of two years,' she explained, frowning at the memory. 'We'd met on the same catering course, would you believe?' She smiled at the memory. 'He was good fun. He wanted to be a TV chef, make a name for himself.' Amy sighed. 'Backroom catering wasn't good enough for Freddie. He tried it for a while but he really felt that he was too big for just cooking behind the scenes. He could have carried on with his training, gone to work for a big cheese in the hotel business, climbed up the ladder like any other aspiring chef, but Freddie wanted it all and he wanted it sooner than yesterday.'

Rafael was intrigued in spite of himself.

'At first, I just found it funny that he was so obsessed with wanting to make it big, but then we started arguing about it. I hated that. My sisters were very wary of him but I clung on until he dumped me.'

Rafael heard the catch in her voice and didn't have to see her to know that her face would be clouding over. She had the sort of face that clouded over. 'You were well rid of him.'

'Well, yes, but still…he dumped me by text message! Said that he'd found someone else. Later I discovered that the *someone else* was twice his age and loaded! He lives in Italy now. He has a brand-new restaurant. Maybe I'll drop in one day and give him the fright of his life.'

'So…then you met James…'

'At work. He made me laugh.'

And he was safe, Rafael worked out. Having a crush on the boss was like hankering behind the impossible, which was why it had only ever remained a crush. Had she decided to take it one step further now that she had seen with her own two eyes exactly how much money was wrapped up in him?

'He makes a lot of people laugh.' Rafael shrugged. 'Did you think that you were special because of that?'

'No, I did not!' Amy flushed guiltily.

'Because you would be a fool if you had.'

'I really don't need you preaching to me when you don't know the first thing about me and probably not much about James either.'

Rafael reluctantly took a step back. He had a hell of a lot more to say on the subject of why she would be mad to even think about getting involved with his brother. James's idea of the ideal woman was one who played hard and had no desire for commitment on any level. He mixed with the fast crowd, the people who enjoyed winter holidays yachting down the Grenadines and wild parties in country houses. He had only been living in London for a matter of a few years but in that short time he had accumulated more contacts than most people did in their entire lifetime. It was James's gift, why he was so brilliant at what he did. But she was on the defensive and that was not where he wanted her.

He brought the subject back to her catering, which seemed a natural topic of conversation as he began to unpack the individual packets of food.

'You don't do this often, do you?' Amy eventually said, interrupting her own monologue, which, to her ears, was beginning to sound like a very boring CV for a job interview. She couldn't think he could possibly be interested.

'Do what?' Rafael looked across at her. She was on all fours and leaning towards him as she inspected the contents of a disposable tub. There he went again, being distracted by her breasts, the shadow of her cleavage, their neat plumpness. He frowned, annoyed with himself, and looked away.

'Have picnics.' She looked up at him. 'I mean,' she clarified, 'you bought loads of spreads but nothing to spread them *with,* and bread but nothing to cut it with, and what are we supposed to put all this stuff *on*?'

Rafael was nonplussed.

'Very boring, you know. I mean, you don't *look* boring,' she hastened to add, feeling a little odd quiver as she stared into those infuriatingly dark sunglasses, 'but I guess you're just not accustomed to eating outdoors. Weird, considering your line of work!'

'Maybe I think it might be a bit of a busman's holiday to spend yet more time outdoors when most of my time is spent there anyway. Mowing lawns. Weeding. Felling the occasional tree.'

Amy frowned. Was he laughing at her? She thought she had been making a perfectly sensible observation.

'In fact, this isn't my idea of fun at all,' he told her bluntly. 'Too much sun, too little shade, sand in the sandwiches.' He stood up and Amy scrambled to her feet. 'I suggest we hop in the car and see where the wind takes us. We can eat something on the way. Somewhere.' Rafael couldn't quite believe his own ears.

Amy gave him a brilliant smile. 'Okay. But what about the food? I mean, it must have cost quite a bit and you didn't let me pay…perhaps I could treat you to lunch? I know you have better things to do than ferry me around because I was stupid enough to land up on your doorstep last night.'

'Perhaps.'

Four hours later, Rafael had to admit that he was enjoying himself. As novel experiences went, spending time in the company of a woman who had no particular interest in the news, no knowledge of the opera, little experience of the theatre and an unhealthy interest in reality television was an eye opener. There was no intellectual conversation about the state of the country, the world economy, and, certainly in the case of Elizabeth, the frustrations of the American legal system.

Instead he had fielded off a thousand intrusive questions about himself, heard all about her chaotic, massive family and discovered, by the time they had made it back to his house, that he had not actually learnt anything at all about her intentions towards his brother. Which had been the whole point of the exercise. And now she was demanding to leave.

'Why?'

'Because people will be wondering where I am.' Amy ticked off all the reasons on her fingers. 'Because there are all sorts of games laid on for this evening and it should be fun. Because I can't stay wearing the same clothes indefinitely.'

Rafael was forced to concede defeat but, having accomplished precisely nothing during the course of the day, he decided, there and then, that he would simply have to put his work on hold for a couple more hours and entertain the woman the following day. It would all be for a good cause.

'Games…' Rafael could think of nothing worse.

'Yup. Casino night. Of course, not with real money, but should be a laugh.'

Rafael grunted. 'Okay. Hop back in the car. I'll take you to the house.'

Amy, strangely disappointed, sat in silence for the short duration of the drive.

'I'll drop you off by the gates, if you don't mind.' He pressed a button on his key ring and the gates slowly inched their way open.

'Guess it'll be a bit uncomfortable for you…' he insinuated casually, killing the engine and leaning back against the door to look at her. The sun had brought her out in a light sprinkling of freckles and, combined with the lack of make-up, made her look very young, very defenceless. James had not paid her a bit of attention, it would seem, since she had started working for the company, but he would be seeing her in a new light here and very young and defenceless could prove a winning combination for him, even if he *did* have a girl lurking in the background. Knowing James, whoever it was would be a temporary fling, easily discarded.

Amy, as he had discovered throughout the course of the day, might not have the striking model looks his brother favoured, but she had an open, infectiously gregarious personality that could be just as lethally attractive.

'I mean, being around your boss…knowing that he's got another woman, that he really hasn't the time of day for you…'

'Thank you very much.'

'Especially when you'd invested time and energy spinning fantasies about getting him into bed…' He didn't like the image in his head of her in bed with his brother, not at all.

Amy was torn between indignation at his assumptions and sheepishness at how accurate they were. Yes, she *had* wasted time and energy spinning fantasies, not to mention a fair amount of money on a certain wardrobe that seemed intent on self-destruction. Probably fate's way of making sure no one looked at her twice. Not even, she brooded, the gardener sitting next to her. Not once had she seen him give her that once-over that was the age-old sign of a man's attraction to a member of the opposite sex. Not once!

'I'm not *that* sad!' Amy lied. 'Anyway, there are lots of people around. It's not as though I shall be forced to talk to him if I don't want to.'

'And would you want to…?'

'Would I want to what?'

'Talk to him. Or are you all over that now?'

She flushed. With the benefit of cruel hindsight and unfortunate, inevitable disillusionment, Amy could see all too clearly that, not only was she cured of her misguided infatuation, but that the infatuation had never been more than a temporary balm to her ego after Freddie. She had been dumped in the most mortifying way possible, never mind that she herself had been thoroughly fed up with him, and the occasional flirting with James had been a pleasant way of passing the time while she recovered her spirit. She had no idea what she might have done had James actually turned around and expressed a desire to get into bed with her.

'Women don't just *get over* broken hearts in the space of a few hours!' she remonstrated, wriggling out of a direct answer.

'Your heart wasn't *broken*. Did you think of the man once during the course of the day?'

'Of course I did!' *Not once!* 'Not,' she emphasised, 'that it's any of your business!'

Rafael thought that she might well be surprised if she knew just how much of his business it was. 'Because,' he murmured, 'I thought you might want to take a bit of time out and spend the day in Manhattan tomorrow…'

He dangled the carrot in front of her and watched her contemplate the tasty bait. She had never been abroad. This was the first time she had stepped foot outside the country. There had always been too many children for her parents to contemplate the expense. He had learnt all this during the course of the day.

'Don't be silly,' Amy told him, dragging her mind away from thoughts of skyscrapers and Central Park, which she had seen on television a million times. 'You can't possibly just take time off whenever you want. I know you probably call the shots with your staff, but don't you think your boss might be a bit miffed if he realises that you're leaving them to their own devices for two days on the trot? You might just be pushing his generosity and I wouldn't want to land you in any trouble.'

'That's very considerate of you,' Rafael said, amused, 'but there's no need to concern yourself on my behalf. The boss and I have a very…amicable relationship. Of course, if you'd rather not…' He found that he *wanted* her to. The realisation was short-lived but overpowering.

'I suppose it *might* be a relief not to be in James's company, knowing that I've made a fool of myself…' She remembered that she was a woman of substance and still reeling with disappointment from Love's Cruel Blow. 'And it would be hard to see him, knowing what I know and yet still…wanting him…'

This was not what Rafael wanted to hear. 'Still wanting him' implied the possibility of ongoing pursuit the minute they were back in England and circumstances had reverted to their normal status quo. It would be evident that whoever had been at the receiving end of James's attentions in the Hamptons would no longer be around and for all she thought that she had been an invisible presence, she might well be surprised to discover that that had not been the case. What normal, red-blooded male could fail to notice her understated appeal? She might not have legs up to her armpits or breasts that announced themselves minutes before their owner arrived, but her sense of humour was irreverent and infectious and her personality was vibrantly captivating. As far as James would be concerned, Rafael amended to himself. He liked fun-loving. The fact that this one came in a different, vastly more intelligent package could well make the difference between a passing affair and a marriage proposal. Rafael couldn't think of that slim possibility without a surge of rage washing over him and an immediate and overwhelming determination to prevent it at all costs.

'So I take it that's a *yes...*'

He collected her at eight-thirty promptly the following morning. Amy had been up and ready since seven. She was back to her jeans, but this time twinned with a small, tight vest-top and her gorgeous new shoes. She had a date with the gardener, she told Claire breezily, who was secretly relieved that she had given up her pointless pursuit of James, and contented herself with only a couple of questions. Notably how she could manage to meet a guy in the space of twenty-four hours, but then she knew the answer well enough. Amy had a sunny personality that people were drawn to, even though she was merrily unaware of the fact. She was also cuter than she thought, with her wild blonde hair and big blue eyes giving her a gamine appeal that many men found captivating. She was far more suited to dates with a gardener than dreaming about the impossibly rich playboy James who represented everything that was unreliable about the opposite sex.

'Bring me back a souvenir,' Claire told her.

'Only if it can be really tacky!' Amy laughed.

'And don't fall for the gardener,' her friend warned, uneasily aware that there was something different about her. 'It would be hard to commute from London to New York three times a week.'

'Believe me,' Amy said sincerely, 'there's no chance of

that!' She thought of Rafael. He might have smouldering good looks, but he was not easy company. She found herself trying to explain the conundrum to Claire until she was interrupted.

'Okay, okay, I get the picture! Though why you would want to spend time with someone you find hard going, I have no idea. That's not like you *at all.*' Curiouser and curiouser, Claire thought. She refrained from saying anything but wondered if jumping out of the frying-pan and straight into the fire would do her friend any good.

Amy rattled off the excuse provided by Rafael and which she had eagerly adopted as her own. 'I'd rather not be around James just at the moment. I feel like an utter fool, to be honest. I mean, it's not as though I haven't *known* that he's had women, but I suppose seeing it for myself up close and personal just really brought it home to me. I've been an idiot, Claire.'

Claire made indeterminate noises that might have been agreement or might have been denial. Fortunately, her friend did not ask for clarification.

'So I just think it would work for me not to be around him too much here if I can help it, and no one's really going to notice because we can all do our own thing if we want to. I mean…*you* could come out with us today if you want…' She found herself guiltily hoping that her friend would turn down the offer, as she did, then she felt guilty that she could have been so selfish. She should *want* Claire around to dilute the sheer get-under-her-skin nature of Rafael's personality.

'Well, you won't be missing much,' Amy said stoutly when Claire declined. 'It's not as though the gardener's a shed load of fun. I mean, the only time he laughs is when he's laughing *at* me!'

'But he's good-looking…' Claire said thoughtfully.

'Not my type. You know I like the fun-loving sorts…and, *yes,*' she continued irritably when Claire raised her eyebrows and grinned, 'I suppose some people might find him handsome…not *cute,* I hasten to add. In fact, he's about as *cute* as a man-eating shark, but I suppose he gets a couple of looks when he goes out…' A couple of hundred, she thought, recalling the heads that had swung around to get a glimpse of him. 'But then he *would,'* she said. 'All that manual outdoor work…rippling muscles everywhere…but not a very *sensitive* kind of guy…' she added.

'So why do you think he's taking a day off just to ferry you around New York?' Claire asked with lively interest.

'Maybe he feels sorry for me,' Amy said, frowning. She couldn't really imagine Rafael feeling sorry for anyone. 'I did lay it on a bit thick about my broken heart.'

'Maybe,' Claire told her with drama in her voice, 'he's fallen for the charms of the beautiful Amy…'

Amy felt the colour start from the tips of her toes and work its way up. The laughter disappeared from her voice instantly. 'That's a ridiculous idea,' she said huriedly.

'But he's spending a whole day with you, even though he doesn't have to…'

'Maybe he just likes the idea of going out with someone from The Big House…'

'Even though he knows that you're not made of money?'

'Who knows what makes the man tick?' Amy said irritably, looking at her watch. 'Who cares?' She wanted to clear off before James came down for breakfast. She didn't want to be answering a series of questions from him about where she was going and with whom, not that he would probably even notice her sitting in front of her plate of half-eaten croissant and streaky bacon. She thought about that and, 'hrrmphed,' in irritation at how pathetic she had been, never mind that she had been recovering from Freddie, who hadn't actually been *worth* recovering from anyway!

And she didn't want to hang around answering Claire's questions. Normally, she would have been the first to have a laugh at her unexpected date, but not, for some reason, this time.

She excused herself, returned to her room and didn't emerge for another half an hour, at which time she sneaked out of the house and found herself running down to the gates at the bottom of the ridiculously long and winding drive.

Which was why, when she saw the sports car waiting for her, her heart was racing. It was just the exertion of the run.

CHAPTER FIVE

RAFAEL was not in the best of moods. Having had a telephone conversation with his brother the night before regarding a hiccup with one of their prospective deals, he had somehow ended up admitting to James that he would be taking Amy out for the day and, because he could not reveal the reason why, had had to endure an inordinate amount of laughter and a lengthy and unedifying lecture on the wisdom of taking a break from the boring power-suited women he usually dated.

As if that hadn't been bad enough, news of his departure from the norm had spread with the speed of light, and at a stupidly early hour this morning he had received an unexpected telephone call from his mother. He had seen through her initial pleasantries in roughly two seconds and then had stuck the phone on loudspeaker and for the duration of the call had actually had time to cook himself some breakfast, download a couple of e-mails and change.

Anyone would think, Rafael thought ill humouredly, that he had decided to book a flight to the moon. When he had casually mentioned that there must be very little of interest happening in his mother's life if she could get excited over something as small as him taking a woman out for the day, he had had to suffer through an amused, pithy speech on how much good it would do him to do something unexpected for once.

'When was the last time you actually took time off work on the spur of the moment?' she demanded.

Rafael diplomatically refrained from telling her that spontaneous breaks from work just whenever the mood grabbed him wouldn't exactly be in the best interests of the company that he ran with such stunning success. Instead, he said, 'About a week ago when I found myself caretaking James...'

'Oh, but that was on the spur of *my* moment,' his mother was quick to point out. He couldn't win.

'What on earth are you wearing?' he asked, as soon as Amy was in the car.

'Jeans,' Amy told him. 'And good morning to you too.'

Rafael looked at the strip of bare midriff on display and grunted. 'They're very low.'

'And you sound like someone's father when you say stuff like that. This is the style.'

'Really. And that would be according to...?'

'According to anyone under the age of thirty...which I guess rules you out...'

And so here we go again, Amy thought, like two combatants circling each other, taking quick punches whenever the opportunity arise. She closed her eyes and let the breeze whip through her hair. Curiously, she felt excited and happy, even though sniping really wasn't her style. She half opened her eyes and peeked at him. The dark sunglasses were in place again and he was driving with one hand on the steering wheel, the other resting lightly on the gearbox. She would never have thought that a gardener would suit a low-slung, convertible sports car, but he did. The latent power of the car fitted him somehow.

'I haven't even seen you in a pair of jeans!' she said, pulling herself together.

'Because I don't own a pair.'

'Everyone owns a pair of jeans!'

Rafael shrugged. That was a fair enough assertion. He wondered how she would react if he told her that he had accounts at New York's most exclusive stores and a personal shopper who kitted him out in whatever he needed. He had neither the time nor the inclination to drift from store to store in search of trendy clothing. He did not possess any jeans because he had never expressed any particular desire to own a pair. Consequently, his casual trousers were hand-tailored but just in less formal and more wearable fabric than his suits. He didn't have to look at her face to know that her expression would be one of horrified fascination at someone whose fashion style resided somewhere in the dinosaur era.

Rafael, who generally didn't give one hoot what other people thought of him, found himself scowling.

'Hmm. No jeans. Maybe we should do a bit of shopping today,' Amy said mischievously. 'Get you looking a little less like an old fuddy duddy.'

'You think I look like a fuddy-duddy?' Rafael shot her a crooked smile and Amy blinked. *No!* He mightn't wear jeans but the last thing this man was was a fuddy-duddy! Her mouth went dry and she could feel her heart speed up. What was going on? she thought, panicked.

'No. I just think it's odd that you don't possess a pair. Anyway, I don't want to go shopping. It was just a joke. I don't actually *care* what you wear or what you own…'

'No…?' Rafael thought about what had brought him out today, playing truant for the first time in his life. He wanted to make sure that when she left the Hamptons she left behind all thoughts of his brother. 'Shame…'

Amy thought that she might have misheard. 'Sorry?' She cleared her throat. God, but that one little word had sent a shameful thrill racing through her and she couldn't understand it.

'I thought all women cared what people thought of them,' Rafael said mildly.

'Oh. Yes. No!'

'I think shopping would be a very good idea,' he mused. 'After all, you can't visit Manhattan and *not* shop.' Under normal circumstances, he would have arranged with his secretary to take a couple of hours off work and show her the wonders that were the shopping districts of Manhattan. Failing that, he realised that he would have to take her himself, which might not be such a bad thing if getting to know her was his primary concern. Problem was that he had no idea where women went shopping in the city.

'I can buy you a pair of jeans,' Amy said, warming to the idea.

'You really think I need some, do you?' Rafael drawled.

'Absolutely!' Sometimes when he spoke the timbre of his voice was curiously sexy. Was he aware of that? He gave no inkling that there was a streak of vanity running through him, but surely he couldn't miss the furtive glances other women directed at him? Could he? 'And maybe a jazzy shirt as well instead of all those plain coloured ones you seem to like wearing…'

He grinned and wondered how she would react if she only knew the cost of those 'plain-coloured ones'! Each was hand tailored. Every six months he would dispose of one lot and replace with another. It might be boring but it was damned convenient.

'Jazzy?'

'Hawaiian print perhaps?' Amy amused herself by imagining him in a ridiculous ensemble. It helped still her nervous awareness of him that had either been there all along or else had crept up on her when she was least expecting it. 'Maybe something with large, bright flowers. That would make a change from dull old white or cream! Thank goodness you don't work in an office. I bet you'd have lots of pinstriped suits to add to your collection!'

Just the odd thirty or so, Rafael thought wryly.

'Here's the deal,' he told her lazily. 'You can shove me in something casual and I'll dress you the way a woman *should* be dressed.'

'The way a woman *should* be dressed?'

'Oh, yes. No jeans that look as though they've been attacked with a pair of scissors...'

'That's *how* they're supposed to look!'

'And I pay for the lot...'

'No way!' She flushed. 'That just wouldn't be right. I mean, it's not as though we're going out. Not that that would make any difference. I don't believe in a man paying for everything.'

'Oh. You mean you're one of those feminist types who insist on splitting everything straight down the middle? What if you had been dating the boss? Would you still have insisted on going Dutch?'

'That would have been different.'

'Why?'

'I know this is going to sound as though I've got a different set of rules, but James has a lot of money. If I had been dating him...' she shuddered at the thought '...I would happily have let him treat me to stuff. After all, I'm broke and he's not. I would have paid him back in my own way.'

'Why don't you enlighten me?' Rafael asked tightly.

Oblivious to his change of tone, Amy gave the question serious thought. 'I would have cooked him special meals... bought him little things that might have meant something to him… There are ways of showing appreciation that can't be counted in financial terms. It's a relative thing, isn't it? I mean, a rich guy can throw money at a woman without missing it while the woman might only be able to afford something very small in comparison but it would mean a whole lot more because she would have to have saved to afford it in the first place.'

'And you think that the gardener couldn't possibly afford to splash out now and again…'

'Maybe you can, but why should you? You barely know me.'

'I've recently had a pretty generous bonus from the master,' Rafael said gravely. 'Humour me.'

'Okay, but no strings attached.'

'What kind of strings?'

'You know what I'm talking about.'

'Do I? Why don't you fill me in?'

'If…you might want to buy me an outfit because you don't think I look feminine enough…'

'Did I say that?'

'Well, no, but…'

'Actually, I think you're incredibly feminine,' Rafael contradicted. And one of the most endearingly feminine things she did was blush. As she was doing right now. Hardened career women, he realised, didn't blush. Or at least none of the ones he had dated in the past. Amy might speak her mind with no respect for boundaries, but she still blushed like a teenager. He decided to rescue her from her embarrassment. 'But if you want to put me in jeans, then I'll put you in a skirt.'

So it was settled. Between Long Island and Manhattan, he managed to unearth the names of some cheap and cheerful stores in Soho. The painful part of the day, he decided to get past first. This entailed Rafael, scraping together every ounce of control, trying on a variety of jeans, which she seemed to find hilarious. After the fifth shop and the eight pair, he decided to put his foot down and threatened to buy the next pair he tried on whether it fitted or not. Amy reluctantly chose. She had been enjoying herself. He looked completely different in jeans. Younger. Sexily dangerous in a more earthy, straightforward way. It should have been the other way around. He should have lived in jeans, just as she did, but there was no accounting for taste.

As she watched him pay she could feel something shifting under her, some conviction altering and morphing into something else, but she shoved the uneasy thought to one side and concentrated on enjoying the day.

She had brought spending money with her and she had given it to him before they had even left Long Island, so she didn't feel guilty when he bought her an ice cream and, later, lunch, which they ate quickly because she wanted to explore as much as she could before they headed back.

She had questions about everywhere and everything, Rafael noticed with amusement. He was blasé to the charms of New York. In fact, he barely noticed them, so it was refreshing to see things a little differently for once.

'Do you ever wish you lived in New York instead of in your little house on someone else's land?' she asked at one point, and Rafael thought of his magnificent penthouse apartment overlooking Central Park. He felt a twinge of guilt and adroitly changed the subject.

It was time for her to fulfill her half of the deal, he told her, and then he would take her to dinner. This time she insisted on paying, thankful that she had brought her credit cards with her.

'I can't afford to take you to the sort of place this kind of outfit requires…' she said dubiously, because the elegant deep red-halter necked dress reeked of somewhere chic. But it was so lovely. Amy realised how entrenched she had become in her casual lifestyle. Catering required no thought when it came to clothes and she never went anywhere that demanded formal dress. She could feel her eyes blurring when she walked out to show him the fit.

'What's the matter?' Rafael asked, startled, tilting her face up.

'Nothing.' Amy's voice was wobbly but she steadied herself and plastered her usual cheerful smile on her face. It wouldn't have fooled an idiot.

'I don't think there's any need to try anything else on. We'll take this one.'

'And what,' he asked as soon as they were outside, 'was that all about?'

But by now Amy's brief glimpse of loss had passed. 'The shock of seeing myself in a dress brought on a sudden attack of the maudlin,' she laughed. 'I was always the tomboy in the family. My sisters dressed like prom queens the minute they turned sixteen whereas I never really left my jeans behind.'

'And you wear them because they remind you of your tree-climbing days?' Rafael had a sudden, startling insight into her. Wearing that dress had shown her a vision of a world he was pretty sure she seldom visited. He didn't know whether that made her more vulnerable to the charms of what money could buy and he didn't care. He just had an insane desire to take her somewhere fancy for dinner. Some place where jeans would not be welcome. He thought of his apartment and the supply of appropriate clothes waiting there for him.

'We need to find somewhere to change,' he said abruptly. 'We'll end the day by going somewhere decent to eat.'

'All this to save me from the trauma of having to face James?' Amy remembered Claire's questions earlier that day when she had asked *why*. *Why* had the gardener, to whom she wasn't attracted and who wasn't attracted to her, decided to put himself out to take her to Manhattan? He didn't *act* as though he was interested in her, but just in case he started getting the wrong idea Amy decided to set him straight.

'All this stuff,' she began awkwardly.

'Stuff?'

'The dress. Now dinner. I hope you don't think that…'

'That…?' Rafael guided her into a coffee shop where she gratefully dropped into a chair. Only problem was that she was now obliged to look him in the face when she talked to him. Very bad. Judging from the innocently curious expression on his face he wasn't about to make things easy for her. Someone came to take their order and seemed excessively cheerful considering their modest request for two cups of unadorned filter coffee when the menu suggested that anything short of a latte was sacrilege.

Rafael leant forward and proceeded to give her the full benefit of his undivided attention.

Vaguely alarmed, Amy inched back and tried to get her scattered thoughts in order. What had she been thinking?

'You were saying…?' he asked with interest. 'Shall I help you out?' he volunteered into the growing silence and Amy gave a strangled response and a shrug that could have meant anything.

He took it to mean that he could embarrass her further by leaning closer. 'You don't want me to think that I'm buying *you* because I'm buying you a cheap dress and something to eat… Not only am I a dinosaur out of touch with the real world, but I'm also caught up in the old-fashioned male way of thinking that dinner equals sex.'

'No! That's not what I meant!'

'Isn't it?'

Amy took refuge in a mouthful of coffee. Why had they come to a coffee shop? Why not a wine bar where she could have gulped back some restorative wine and found a bit of

Dutch courage to continue the conversation? 'Well, you can't blame me, can you? I mean, it's only fair to lay one's cards on the table from the outset. That way there won't be any misunderstandings and a girl has to look out for herself, don't you agree?' She wondered, in panic, how she could have the nerve to warn off a man most women would throw themselves at. No wonder his expression was one of surprised disbelief. She sternly reminded herself that it was imperative to lay down her ground rules irrespective of what he looked like.

'What makes you think that you're my type?'

Amy's mortification deepened. Rafael thought that she really did blush extremely well. Granted, James would probably only have seen her in her working clothes and his imagination led him to believe that her working clothes would be far from sexy, but how was it that his brother hadn't been able to glimpse the tantalising woman behind the uniform? Rafael was slightly surprised considering James prided himself on his vast knowledge of the opposite sex.

'I'm not your type any more than you're mine,' she said, thinking on her feet, 'but I just don't want any misunderstandings to occur.'

'What *is* your type?' Rafael asked. 'James, I suppose?'

Amy, in that split second, had a moment of terrible realisation. James wasn't her type even though she had sincerely thought he was, even though he really was the sort of guy she usually went for, a guy who had the gift of the gab and didn't take life too seriously. Yes, of course, they worked hard but they always knew how to have a good time. Guys like Freddie and those before him all the way down the years to when she had been a teenager dating the captain of the school sports team. If anyone had told her that she might one day be drawn to a man who hardly ever seemed to smile, never mind laugh, who didn't possess a pair of jeans and with a CD collection she would hate to see, she would have laughed until she cried.

All her boyfriends had been blond, for heaven's sake! It was a standing joke in her family. How dared this cynical dark-haired man sneak up on her from behind and get under her skin?

As she was still reeling from the thunderbolt, something else wormed its way out of hiding and filled her consciousness like a dangerous, toxic fog. Not only was she attracted to this least likely of men, but this least likely of men could prove to be the most lethal to her system because she reacted to him in a way she had never reacted to any boy or man in her life before. It was as if he made her three-dimensional. He could hurt her and Amy didn't want to be hurt. She could see now that she had never been hurt before, not really, not in any meaningful way.

'That's right. James. He's my type.' How on earth could she be attracted to a man who rubbed her up the wrong way most of the time? Who seemed to enjoy silently laughing at her? 'I've always been a sucker for blonde hair,' she babbled on, staring at Rafael and feeling all her foundations swaying dangerously beneath her. He was sinfully sexy. How could she have blithely assumed that she would be immune to that just because he didn't fit her norm? 'Some people are like that, aren't they? I've always gone for the fair-haired guy.' She tried to look wistful, amused and sincere all at the same time. 'I bet you're the same.' She pretended to scrutinise him. It was horribly easy to lose herself in the dark, rugged masculinity of his face. There was nothing pretty about him. Every feature was strongly delineated, from the slashing cheekbones and angular nose to the curving mouth and raven-dark hair swept away from his face. He was all man without benefit of moisturisers, hair gel or expensive cologne. She realised that she was losing track of what she was saying in the process of inspection, and she cleared her throat. 'I bet…' she drew out the syllables in a comical impersonation of a B-rated movie detective '…you go for brunettes. Yes. Outdoorsy brunettes who love nothing better than hiking up the side of a mountain or running in marathons. The sort who believe that make-up is a sin against Nature.' She laughed, although she could feel her heart beating fast and her eyes drinking in his face, memorising every line for future reference.

'James is not noted for his good reputation as far as women are concerned…'

'Why do you keep acting as though you know him intimately?' Although she was well aware that his track record wasn't good. He surfaced frequently in the gossip columns of tabloid newspapers and there was always a dishy, leggy blonde on his arm. Now Amy knew why that had never particularly troubled her in the past, even though she had made all the right disgruntled noises to Claire. Because he had never really got under her skin. Not like this man.

'Doesn't that bother you?' Rafael persisted.

'Why should it?' Amy said carelessly.

'You mean you're that convinced of your charms…?'

'Oh, well—the way I see it is like this: James goes out with stereotypes. They're all tall, they're all blonde and they all look like they've stepped off the cover of *Vogue* magazine. So maybe he might be dazzled by the fact that I'm different…' The theory, not that it mattered, was only now occurring to her, but, thinking about it, it made sense. She decided to elaborate on it as a means of backtracking from her embarrassing assertion that they should lay their cards on the table. As a way, too, of covering up the shocking revelation that the sexy images in her head had nothing to do with James.

'I mean, think about it…' She didn't think that she had ever seen such fathomless dark eyes. A woman could lose herself in them. A fair few probably had and she wondered, jealously, what they had been like. Mountain-climbing amazons, as she had implied? 'He might be bowled over by the novelty of a woman who bears no resemblance to anything from the cover of any magazine...'

Bowled over by the novelty...

Rafael was forcibly struck by the significance of her passing phrase. He didn't know whether this was a theory she was working on or whether she had come to the Hamptons with the express purpose of putting it into practice, only to be derailed by finding him with another woman. Certainly, in either case it was a plan waiting in the wings for opportunity to meet circumstance.

Something bristled inside him. James was a big boy and he could look after himself, but Rafael could feel the stirring of intent begin to crystallise inside him. He had been sent to the Hamptons on a mission to babysit his brother. His mother had been thinking of a far more straightforward babysitting job, but he was pretty sure that she would feel the same as he did now. That Amy must be kept away from James and remain that way. Permanently.

His mobile phone vibrated and he excused himself, using the opportunity to pay the bill at the counter, snapping it shut as he approached her.

'Don't tell me...' Amy stood up, her smile bright, over-bright, her eyes making a point of not leaving his face. 'Your boss. Checking to make sure that you'll be back out to work tomorrow, just in case your head gets turned by all the exciting things happening in Manhattan.' She pictured him wearing the faded, low slung jeans she had insisted he buy and once the image was in her head, found it very difficult to release.

Rafael murmured something that could have passed for agreement. 'Oh, I think James knows what a loyal...employee I am,' he said with a straight face. 'In fact,' he continued as they headed outside, straight into the furnace blast of pure New York summer, 'I told him that we were overrunning on time and he very kindly offered us the use of the company apartment if we wanted to change before going out for a meal tonight...' Well, today had certainly brought out a side to him he had never before explored. Work, a first for him, had taken a back seat and now he was about to lay the groundwork for seduction. The seduction of a woman who had stated, categorically, that she didn't find him attractive.

Rafael was beginning to realise just how simple his love life had previously been. He met women easily, either through friends or more usually in the course of work. Elizabeth he had met over a deal and their shared interests in the vagaries of company law had led to a relationship that had trundled on quite nicely for a while. He had never had to work at a relationship and he had certainly never had to persuade a woman into bed.

But the challenge of unknown territory sent an alien excitement through him. It was something like the thrill he got at the start of a new and complex deal, one that might work or might not, but this excitement had the added edge of sexual conquest, and loathsome though it was for him to view any woman in those terms, he couldn't help the primitive kick of undiluted adrenaline that was pumping through his body. The unsophisticated concept of the chase and every cavemanlike instinct associated with it was proving to be an irresistible turn-on.

'What...?' He realised that he hadn't heard a word she had been saying to him.

'I *said,*' Amy repeated very slowly, 'I think we ought to be getting back to the house. It's...rude for me to abandon the party when everything has been laid on especially. Not especially for *me,* of course, but for all of us here. Not that I'm not grateful to you for taking my mind off…things…' what a crazy piece of irony, she thought '…but…'

'But you're scared…'

Amy froze, hands on hips, and glared at him. 'Scared of *what*?' He had carried on walking. Now he turned around and slowly walked back towards her. Even his economical, graceful movements were peculiarly mesmerising.

'Of wearing that dress I bought for you…'

Of all the inaccurate things he could have said, that took the biscuit. Amy burst out laughing. 'I'd love to wear the dress!' she told him. 'I *never* wear dresses. I always wear trousers or skirts. But, believe me, I'm not scared of getting into a dress just because I also happen to wear jeans!'

'I don't believe you,' Rafael said, as cool as a cucumber, one hand holding the assorted bags, the other shoved deep into his trouser pocket. 'Do you feel you might be out of your depth in a swinging New York restaurant?'

'Because I'm just a lowly nobody from across the Atlantic?' Amy snapped, hurt. 'Isn't that something like the pot calling the kettle black?'

'Oh, New York's my home. And besides, as you pointed out, I have expensive tastes, whatever my profession. Here in New York you'll find that wearing the right clothes is a passport to pretty much anywhere.'

'Oh, and you're really going to fit in wearing jeans or those shorts you've got on!' Unfairly, she thought he probably would.

'No problem. I'll buy something decent.'

'Just like that!' She snapped her fingers and wondered, not for the first time, about the seemingly limitless stream of money he kept tapping into. *She* had no dependants either, but she still always seemed to be counting her pennies and trying to work out finances on scraps of paper.

'Just like that,' Rafael agreed. He never thought about money. He made vast sums of it and therefore had no need to economise in any way whatsoever. The women he had dated in the past, though not in his league at all, had been substantial earners in their own right. Lengthy debates about the price of a pair of shoes were alien to him. And he had always considered himself by far the more laboriously realistic brother! 'But before you turned down my offer without hearing me out, the company flat isn't in use at the moment. I'm not *buying* you, but it's getting late. We might just as well grab something here and you can wear your dress. Unless you'd rather get back early and drink your sorrows away over a makeshift roulette table…?'

Mindful that, to him, he was doing her a good deed, taking her out of herself, and aware that the last thing she wanted would be to give him any inkling that the storm raging inside her had nothing to do with James, Amy gave his proposition some thought. If she really *had* been reeling from a broken heart at finding the love of her life in the arms of another woman, what would she be inclined to do? Mope? She had never moped in her entire life. She had had friends who moped at the end of a love affair and she had always wondered how they could expend so much energy on doing nothing but wandering around under a cloud of depression, seeking out people to whom they could analyse, for hours, why what had happened had happened and how it could have been prevented from happening.

If she *had* been nursing a broken heart, she decided, then, yes, she *would* want to take her mind off things by having a good time, by dressing up and going out. And he *had* bought that red dress for her, even though it hadn't been all that expensive and with her protesting all the way to the checkout till. It seemed churlish now to refuse his offer for dinner. For all she knew he might hardly ever get out! It might even be construed, she thought, that she would be doing him a *kindness* by accepting his invitation.

And of course, she thought with guilty anticipation, she *wanted* to spend time in his company. Oh, it wasn't going anywhere and she wouldn't want it to because, aside from the small technicality of the Atlantic Ocean, he wasn't a *keeper*. He was a free spirit. No ties and none wanted. That was the impression he gave and she was pretty sure she was spot on target. But that was fine because she wasn't looking for a relationship anyway. Just some light-hearted banter and that glorious little sizzle she felt when she looked at him. Also it was fun locking horns with him because the guys she knew were all so frivolous in comparison.

She shrugged and nodded. 'I can't believe the perks you have with your job,' she teased. 'Company flat. Company fantastic house on great grounds doing not very much from the looks of it…'

Rafael laughed and glanced across at her with amused appreciation. The sun was working on her skin, turning it a light, healthy golden colour and streaking her already pale hair with even paler highlights. She was now asking him how often he stayed at the company flat, making joking noises about wanting a company flat herself, but maybe somewhere hot and sunny like the Caribbean.

'I think I've stayed in the flat once,' Rafael said honestly, 'a few years ago.'

'But you have a key?'

'There's porterage. I expect James will call him and warn him of my arrival.'

'Wow.'

Rafael hadn't heard anyone say 'wow' since he was a kid. His lips twitched.

'So we just get there, use the place and then disappear for something to eat?'

'There's always the option of spending the night there,' Rafael said casually and he could feel her visibly tense. Again he felt that primitive kick of arousal. The civilised half of him was disgusted by the reaction but the other half was already rising to a challenge he'd never thought he would seek. Where the hell was the urbane, sophisticated, opera-and theatre-loving man now? he wondered. He reached out, hailing a cab, prepared for the gridlock traffic that almost defeated the point of a taxi.

He guided the conversation back to safe waters, sensing her relax so that by the time they finally arrived at the apartment building, which was old and immaculately kept, away from the main drag of the city, she barely reacted to the idea that they would be alone in an apartment together.

Even when they had stepped out of the taxi and his witty anecdotes about life in New York had temporarily ceased as he paid the cab driver, she still didn't feel any gut-wrenching nerves.

Why should she? she told herself. It had taken her by surprise but it was no crime to be attracted to him. She would be heading back to London in a couple of days and he would be a pleasant memory. The gardener who was not like any gardener she had ever met. A novel experience. One she would forget on the flight over because that was just the nature of things.

If offer card is missing write to: The Harlequin Reader Service, 3010 Walden Ave., P.O. Box 1867, Buffalo, NY 14240-1867

BUSINESS REPLY MAIL
FIRST-CLASS MAIL   PERMIT NO. 717-003   BUFFALO, NY

POSTAGE WILL BE PAID BY ADDRESSEE

HARLEQUIN READER SERVICE
3010 WALDEN AVE
PO BOX 1867
BUFFALO NY 14240-9952

NO POSTAGE
NECESSARY
IF MAILED
IN THE
UNITED STATES

CHAPTER SIX

AMY could hear herself babbling. It was something that usually happened after a couple of glasses of wine, when she was relaxed and expansive in confiding her emotions to whoever happened to be listening. Her friends told her that it was very sweet. She interpreted that, once she had sobered up, to mean that it was an intensely irritating and boring trait that they put up with because they were her friends.

Rafael Vives was not her friend. She wasn't quite sure what he was, but he certainly wasn't her *friend* even though he had bought her a fantastic dress that felt great and looked better, and was now in the process of spending money feeding her. At what appeared to be a very expensive restaurant even though he had assured her that it was in fact very reasonable and part of a chain, making it sound as though it really were on a level with the Pizza Hut she went to every so often for something to eat after work with her friends.

'You need to get out more often,' Amy said suddenly, interrupting herself in mid-flow with a sudden change of topic. She was impressed to see that Rafael didn't bat an eyelid at the abrupt digression. He just topped up her glass and raised his eyebrows enquiringly. He did that very nicely, she thought with tipsy appreciation. Little inclination of the head, slight smile playing on his lips, just a fetching hint of amusement in his expression.

'Why do you say that?'

'Well, all this effort for a stranger?' Amy looked around her. 'I know you've told me that this is some kind of cheap fast food chain—'

'I don't recall describing it as "cheap" or "fast food".'

'Technicality.' Amy waved her hand to dismiss his interruption. 'Fact is…' she leaned towards him and made a very concentrated effort to sound grave and in control of her wayward mouth, which had a tendency to let her down at the best of times, never mind after a couple of drinks '…you didn't have to bring me on this sightseeing tour of The Big Apple…' She frowned. 'Where does that expression come from anyway? The Big Apple? Funny things, expressions…' She propped her chin in the palm of one hand and looked at him thoughtfully. At any rate, thoughtful was the expression she was aiming for rather than gawping, which she felt very much like doing, as she had felt since the night had kicked off two hours earlier with a drink at a trendy bar in downtown Manhattan. She had dressed in her flimsy, sexy red dress, feeling like a million dollars, and he had dressed in something he had bought in the space of five seconds on their way back to James's company apartment. How could a five-second shop produce such a staggering result? she had later wondered.

The black trousers, plain shirt and dark brogues might well have been the sort of outfit that she would have found ridiculously stodgy on a man, but on him it looked fantastic. So even though she had been conscious of him all the time they had been at the apartment, it really hadn't been too bad. The place was enormous, big enough for them to get ready without actually crossing paths, which she was pretty sure would have bothered her a lot more than it would have bothered him. It was only as she had seen him in his full regalia that her heart had gone into insane overdrive.

In that instant, he had stopped being the gardener and turned into someone else. She told herself that the notion was silly because people didn't fundamentally change according to their dress code, but she had still become idiotically tongue-tied and took the fastest route to self-control via a stiff Bloody Mary at bar number one, followed by some wine at bar number two and now at the restaurant.

In a minute she would start slurring her words and nobody could ever say that that was a ladylike way to behave. She took a couple of gulps of mineral water and breathed in deeply.

'Hysterical,' Rafael said, amused.

'What is?'

'Never mind. You were saying? About my decision to introduce you to some of New York?' Rafael marvelled that there could be something so utterly feminine about a woman who had clearly had too much to drink, something he had always found abhorrent in the past. The red shoestring strap of her dress was in the process of slipping off one slender shoulder, despite her valiant efforts to keep it in place, and her hair was everywhere she probably didn't want it to be. She was looking at him very earnestly, so earnestly, in fact, that he suspected she was trying to get her thoughts into some kind of coherent order. He was happy to wait in silence for her because her frowning concentration was mesmerising.

'Yes. Right. Why did you? You never really said.'

Rafael shrugged. 'Why did you accept? You never really said.'

'I hate the way you do that. Answer a question with a question. It's rude. My mum said that if you're asked a question, it's only polite to answer it.'

'I've heard a lot about your mother. I'd like to meet her.'

'She's part Irish and would eat you alive.'

Since no one had ever come close to doing any such thing, Rafael couldn't resist a low laugh. 'Would she now?' he murmured lazily.

'Yes, she would,' Amy informed him testily because he suddenly looked very arrogant and way too big for his boots for her liking.

What a favour he was doing his brother, Rafael thought. If only James knew! This woman could oh, so easily have got her hooks into him because, as Rafael was increasingly seeing for himself, she was far from the ditzy blonde he had originally imagined her to be. In fact, she shared her mother's carnivorous appetite because she would have eaten James alive! James, for all his experience of the opposite sex, would have been putty in Amy's hands, had she managed to get them on him, because underneath that cute blonde exterior she was as sharp as a knife. James's blondes were malleable dolls in comparison. He had no experience of the knife-wielding variety.

'I felt sorry for you,' he told her. 'Making the mistake of falling for the boss isn't a crime in itself—stupid, yes, but not a crime—and being stuck on foreign shores when you happen to realise your stupidity isn't fun, I should imagine. Manhattan seemed a useful antidote.'

Amy tried to sift through his words, suspiciously aware that not many of them were flattering to her.

'Why is it stupid?' she snapped, ruffled at herself for staring at a man who thought she was stupid.

'Because bosses rarely notice minions.' He, certainly, had no idea what the woman who did their catering looked like, if indeed it was a woman.

'Oh, right, and you speak from bitter experience, do you?' Amy sniggered, sensing a perfect opportunity to get back at him. 'Do you have a crush on your boss? Is that why you're cooped up doing his garden instead of living in a house that you own, married with two kids, doing your *own* garden?'

It took a few seconds for Amy's words to sink in, then he couldn't help himself. He laughed until his face ached, until he could feel people staring curiously at him wondering whether he was all right, until tears threatened to roll down his cheeks. Finally, when the laughter had subsided he risked a look at her and laughed all over again at the frosty expression on her face.

Amy waited until he had quite finished. 'I don't know what you find so funny,' she told him, looking down her nose and trying to ignore the way that burst of laughter had made him seem even sexier. 'It's pretty odd that a man like you is still living in someone else's house, doing someone else's gardens.'

'A man like me?'

Amy shrugged and stared down at the remnants of coffee in her cup. For somewhere cheap and cheerful, the restaurant had proved to be top-notch as far as food was concerned, and full of people who looked neither cheap nor, for that matter, particularly cheerful.

'Lots of people fall for their bosses,' she said defensively, because he looked as if he might succumb to another bout of uncontrollable laughter. 'Unscrupulous secretaries are always running off with the men they work for!'

'Are you saying that you're unscrupulous?'

'I'm saying that it's not the most incredible notion in the world for a woman to fall for the guy she happens to work for.'

'You're not James's secretary.' Thank God, Rafael added to himself. He could picture her bending over his desk, exposing a little too much cute little thigh, looking at him with all that blonde curly hair falling over her face, looking young, girlish and wanton all at the same time. A bit like she looked now. He felt his body respond with slamming speed and he shifted in his seat to try and rid himself of his inconvenient erection.

'I realise that,' Amy snapped. 'Oh, I have no idea why I'm having this conversation with you! You would *never* understand!'

'Because I'm not a boss?'

'Well, you *are* a boss…'

'But none of my employees are sexy little pieces…'

Was he referring to her as *sexy?* She gulped back some more water hurriedly and reddened.

'And if they were, I would certainly be attracted to one of them. That's a little Victorian, isn't it? I realise you think I'm a dinosaur, but I'm certainly not a male chauvinist.'

'I didn't say that you were…I'm just defending my… *feelings* for James. Yes, crazy. Yes, stupid, as you so kindly pointed out. But, no, not that unusual.'

'You mean the feelings you *had* for James.'

'Well, it's not really any of your business, is it, Rafael? We keep getting back to this. Why are you so interested in whether I'm after your boss or not, anyway?'

'He's out of your league.'

Amy snapped out of her meandering thoughts and looked at Rafael, shocked. 'Now that *is* an antiquated way of thinking,' she said slowly. 'And I think that it's time we went now if we're to make it back to the house at all tonight.

Rafael paid without argument but as soon as they were out of the restaurant, he turned to her and said abruptly, 'Spit it out.'

'I *thought*,' Amy said, without bothering to pretend that she didn't know what he was talking about, 'tonight that maybe I had been wrong about you. I *thought* that maybe, just maybe, you weren't as *arrogant* and…well…but I was wrong…'

'Because I told you that you were out of his league?' Rafael hailed a yellow cab and Amy allowed herself to be shuffled inside. It was late and the traffic was less ferocious than it had been earlier when they had travelled back to the apartment.

Where, she knew, they were now heading, not least because they both had clothes to collect. His boss might be generous but she didn't think he would be generous enough to allow his employee to set up indefinite camp in the plush company flat. Which brought her thoughts right back to James and Rafael's remark.

'I don't know what it's like over here,' she said coldly, 'but those class distinctions vanished in England a long time ago.' Their eyes tangled. His disbelieving, hers defensive. 'Well, more or less,' she felt obliged to climb down. 'No one feels as though they're stuck in their station in life and there shall they remain for ever!'

'On the other hand,' Rafael pointed out harshly, 'some wealthy men might not share that particular viewpoint.'

'Are you saying that, from your limited experience of your boss, *that* he's a die-hard snob?'

'You're making a scene.' Rafael turned to her, eyes as hard as flint. 'I dislike women who make scenes.'

'And I dislike men who live their lives on generalisations. So there we go. We're even. We dislike each other.'

'You look like a kitten,' Rafael muttered under his breath, 'but you have the claws of a cat.'

Amy, who couldn't make out what he had said but assumed it must be an insult of sorts, continued to glare at him.

'What did you say?' she asked with accusation in her voice. She was darned if she was going to play the silent little lady while he dished out whatever insults happened to fly through his mind!

'I refuse to have a conversation with you until you've calmed down.'

'Oh, for goodness' sake! Are you for real? Don't you know that self-expression is one of the most important ways of clearing the air?' She and her ex-boyfriend used to have noisy and exuberant arguments, which had inevitably ended up with one or the other storming out. Thinking about it, she wasn't too sure whether those rows had ever done anything constructive, but she decided to keep that admission to herself while he sat there, looking at her as though she had taken leave of her senses.

'According to…whom?'

'According to everyone! Pick up any psychology book,' she sniffed, calming down by the second, 'and you'll find them telling you that a good old shout is worth its weight in gold. I know you're the strong, silent, I'll-just-work-out-my-feelings-by-pulling-up-a-few-weeds type, but you *must* have had a few healthy, flaming rows with girlfriends in the past!'

'Never,' Rafael told her calmly.

'Never?'

'I don't find women who shout attractive. It demonstrates lack of control.'

'What sort of women do you go out with?' Amy asked incredulously. Did women really still come in the strong, silent variety? In her experience, most women were emotional creatures who were not backward at expressing their feelings. She didn't think she was out of the ordinary in that aspect, but judging from the way he was staring at her she was. At least in his eyes.

'Women who don't give in to hysteria at the drop of a hat.'

Rafael felt an unholy thrill of enjoyment as she sizzled in teeth grinding silence for a few seconds, then she nodded in apparent comprehension.

'Oh, yes. For a minute there I had to think because most of the women I know actually think that it's a good thing to express their feelings, but now I can see that the type of woman you're talking about are the *boring* types. I've met a few of those in my time—' Amy sniggered '—always frowning at you over their sensible spectacles if you laugh too loudly in a public place or making derogatory remarks about "the youth of today."'

Rafael looked away to avoid the risk of bursting into laughter. When he had controlled the impulse, he stared at her impassively. 'I didn't say that I dated geriatrics,' he said without a flicker of amusement.

'Well, if you didn't *rile me* I wouldn't blow my top!' What sort of women do you date and what do they look like? she wanted to ask. And where on earth do you meet them?

Then it occurred to her. He met them through James. Of course! Why hadn't she thought of it before? No wonder he didn't seem like just any ordinary gardener! He was definitely a cut above the rest and, with his looks and body, he would have no trouble attracting the super-rich bored young things he probably met through his boss, or even—who knew?—the super-rich bored older models he might meet through his boss's mother!

'You fall for inappropriate men. You climb trees in the middle of the night. You say exactly what's on your mind and to hell with the consequences. I think it's fair to say that you're the sort who blows her top without too much provocation.'

Amy would have liked to have taken him up on his 'falling for inappropriate people' accusation. If what she strongly suspected was true, then this was most definitely a case of the pot calling the kettle black. Unfortunately, without evidence, she would be in his direct firing line, especially as he already thought that she said the first thing that came into her head without bothering to think it out first.

'I won't even bother to defend myself against that,' she said loftily. 'You've got your opinions and you're welcome to them.' She sneaked a glance at him and had a sudden vision of him lying naked on that bed of his, spent after love making. He would be a passionate lover. She was sure of it. Dinosaur or no dinosaur. She tossed her head and looked away quickly. 'It's not as though you mean anything to me, anyway.'

The taxi was now outside the apartment building, which made her realise two things. The first was that she hadn't even been aware of the passage of time, so lost had she been in their little spat. The second was that they still hadn't sorted out what was going to happen about returning to the Hamptons.

As if reading her mind, Rafael, with one hand resting on the door handle, turned to her and said, without bothering to sweeten the pill, 'It's far too late to head back to the house now. Sorry.'

Amy catapulted out of the car and counted to ten, then she walked to where he was standing, still doing the gentlemanly thing and paying the cab driver without asking for her share of the trip, and smiled sweetly up at him.

He smiled back down at her and spoke before she had a chance to.

'Well done. Congratulations.'

'What are you talking about?' She tripped after him into the building. After a long evening out, her feet were aching in her new shoes and she slipped them off and held them in one hand, thereby diminishing her height still further.

'You resisted the urge to rant,' he said approvingly. 'Perhaps with time I could yet turn you into one of those so-called boring women who don't give in to every passing temptation to fly off the handle.'

'Well, thank goodness you don't have time on your side,' Amy said with asperity, 'because I can't think of anything worse. Except, that is, for staying at this apartment tonight. Which is out of the question.'

'No choice.' Rafael didn't look at her but he was very much aware of her at his side. For such a diminutive person, she had an overwhelming presence, he was discovering.

'Of course there's a choice.' Now they were in the lift for the three-floor ride up to the apartment. Amy liked it. It lacked the brash *newness* of everything else she had seen in Manhattan that day.

'Yes, you're right, of course.' The lift bumped to a stop and the doors slid open silently.

'I'm glad you agree with me.' Admittedly she was a little surprised that she had won the argument with such little fuss. He might not like scenes, but somehow, without creating any, he always seemed to get his own way.

'The choice is for you to make. Stay here or head back to the big house. On your own. Because I, for one, am going nowhere.' He unlocked the door, pushed it open and strode into the apartment without turning around. If he had, he would have seen that she had not stepped over the threshold. In fact, she stood at the doorway, gaping, like a fish suddenly deprived of water.

'I can't go back there on my own at this hour!'

'Then it looks like you're stuck with me here.'

'That's not fair.'

'On you or on me?'

Amy ground her teeth together in helpless frustration. 'I thought you were a *gentleman*!'

'Which is why I'm now offering you the bigger of the bedrooms.'

Amy badly wanted to rant. Instead, she straightened her back and strode into the apartment because her choice had been no choice at all and she intended to make the best of the situation, which meant, first off, taking that bigger bedroom he had offered, with its en suite bathroom and dressing area.

'I accept.' She headed towards the bedroom, ignoring his surprised silence. Maybe he had expected her to let her pride refuse the offer. 'What time shall we leave in the morning?

Or—' she glanced at him over her shoulder '—would you rather stay here and make me return to the house on my own? Just to test the water, see whether I can live up to your ideal woman who wouldn't dream of creating a scene whatever the hell was thrown at her?'

'Whoever said anything about *ideal*?' Rafael murmured.

'Okay. Maybe not ideal.' Amy had turned around and was looking at him squarely in the face. 'But the sort of woman *you like*. The sort of woman you date, go out with, have a relationship with, fall in love with…' Amy didn't know where all that had suddenly come from. She did, however, know that she would rather she had kept it to herself. She clapped her hand to her mouth and reddened.

Suddenly saving James from his fate, protecting him from a potential gold-digger, became an inconspicuous aim on the distant horizon. Rafael had a disconcerting moment in which he lost all sense of perspective. It was as if the ground had suddenly shifted from under his feet.

'Go to bed,' he said roughly. 'And no. You won't have to make your way back to the house on your own.' He turned away, leaving Amy guiltily aware that her passing remark might have been one invasion too far of his privacy.

He was disgusted with her, she thought miserably. She had a long bath, washing away the effects of the evening, which had been going so well only to fall apart at the end. With the warm water covering her and foam concealing the few bits of her body that were exposed because she had tipped way too much of the bubble bath in, Amy closed her eyes and relived every minute of the day and night they had spent together.

She had accepted his offer to show her around Manhattan and, instead of being grateful because he had been doing her a good turn, had proceeded to give him the full, uninvited benefit of her mind. She had been unnecessarily sarcastic when she should have been thanking him for his attempts to distract her from her humiliation over James. How was he to know that her broken heart had been nothing of the sort? How was he to realise that her extreme reaction to *him* had stemmed from her inappropriate attraction, against all odds?

She squeezed the sponge and watched the water trickle out of it, making patterns on the surface of the bubbly white foam.

When she thought about it, she realised that she was either chattering to him senselessly and tediously about bits of her life he probably wasn't in the least bit interested in, or else jumping down his throat for things he hadn't said or done.

And then to have laid into him for not obliging her by returning her *immediately and at his inconvenience* to the house! She cringed and sank a little deeper into the bath water.

For a short while she wallowed in a bit of self justification as she remembered his jibe about being out of James's league. Of all the nerve! And he of all people! But then, she thought with a pleasurable injection of spite, if he spent his time bedding the socialites he met through his employees, maybe he felt himself a bit further up the pecking order than her! Ha!

She decided that this train of thought was a lot more comfortable to deal with than the one that involved her beating herself up for being a fool.

She relaxed into a lazy recollection of all the hard work she had put in to become a caterer. Not to mention the parental disappointment she had had to face because both her parents had wanted her to go to university, maybe become a teacher. They had never had the opportunity for further education. They had been keen to instil its importance in all their children from a very young age. Amy had resisted all attempts to manoeuvre her into yet more time spent learning. The thought of years of exams and teaching classrooms of recalcitrant children had brought her out in a cold sweat.

Huh! What had *he* gone through to get his gardening job? she asked herself piously.

Had he spent years training under some Head Gardener somewhere? Had he been made to fall into line with the rose-bush pruning or else face a barrage of abuse? She thought not!

He had probably just turned up, stripped off his shirt to prove that he had the necessary brawn and got the job.

She let her mind wander dangerously over the image of him revealing that necessary brawn and yanked it back into line with a mental slap on the wrist.

Unfortunately doing so also made her pleasantly self-righteous moral high ground disappear like a puff of smoke and she was back where she started. Chastising herself for reacting like a spoiled kid.

It wasn't so much a case of what had he been thinking, daring to tell her that James was out of her league. More a case of what had she been thinking to have jumped down his throat at the well-intentioned and probably very true observation!

With a groan of impatience with herself, Amy dried off and after a moment's thought stuck on the white towelling robe very kindly provided by the anonymous firm that looked after the apartment. Or at least the woman who had kitted it out.

She wouldn't waste time arguing herself out of an apology, she thought, making her mind up with her usual speedy impulsiveness.

She let herself out of the bedroom and padded across the sitting area to where bedroom number two was located.

The apartment had been cleverly arranged. One bedroom with its *en suite* and dressing area lay at the opposite end of the apartment to the second bedroom, which wasn't quite as big and did not lead into an *en suite* or dressing area. It also had all the accoutrements for an office, which meant, she supposed, that anyone from overseas who needed to use the place for any length of time would be able to convert the smaller bedroom into an office, complete with desk, Internet connection, phone, fax machine and all the other boring paraphernalia that every businessman seemed addicted to.

The kitchen, the living area, the dining area—everything was designed in an open-plan fashion so that the feeling was of airiness.

He was up. She could see the fine line of light under the door. Just as well. It was one thing to apologise on the spur of the moment, but something else to wake him up to do it.

Amy took a deep breath and knocked. When, after a few seconds, she heard him tell her to enter, she pushed open the door before she had time to back out.

He was lying on the bed, propped up against the pillows with his laptop computer resting on his thighs. And, aside from a pair of dark, patterned boxer shorts, he was wearing absolutely nothing.

That was fine, she told herself sternly. She was just here to clear the air and then she would be on her way.

'You're working?'

It dawned on her that it was a bit strange for the gardener to be working on a laptop computer at nearly midnight, but her question was answered when he snapped shut the lid and casually told her that he was just catching up with some personal correspondence.

Amy licked her lips nervously.

'Right. Well…'

'You can come in,' Rafael said. 'I don't bite.' He slid the laptop next to him and folded his arms behind his head, all the better to observe her embarrassed dithering by the bedroom door.

The towelling robe she was wearing had clearly been destined for a much larger wearer because it engulfed her.

'What do you want?' he asked brusquely, slinging his feet over the side of the bed and strolling towards the window so that he could perch on its broad sill. Somehow being in bed while she stood there felt just a little...*unsettling*.

Amy drew in a deep breath and said in a rush, 'I came to apologise. For flying off the handle and being...well...a bit of a misery to be with after all you've done for me today.' She ventured nervously into the room so that she didn't have to deliver her speech like someone on stage. 'I showed up on your doorstep and you could have just dumped me back at the house, but you listened to me babble away and you even volunteered to bring me to Manhattan to spare me the discomfort of being in James's company last night.' She could feel herself really getting on a roll now.

Rafael resisted the urge to tell her that it hadn't been the world's greatest sacrifice. An unusual good deed from him, true enough, but he had had his reasons and as things turned out had ended up having a...memorable time, despite the anticlimax of the evening.

Amy took a few tentative steps towards him.

'I don't think I've even really said *thank you* for...the dress...and the tour guide...and...' She wondered whether she should start listing all the cabs he had paid for, not to mention the food they had eaten.

Rafael held up his hand to stop her in mid-flow. 'I get the general picture.'

'And you were right.'

'Was I? What about?' Sometimes trying to follow her conversation was like trying to hang on to running water. And she was now standing pretty close to him. Too close. He clenched his teeth together and pinned his eyes to her tremulous mouth, anything to stop them from straying to the opening of the towelling robe, which was revealing slightly more than she probably thought.

'When you told me that I was out of James's league…' She came closer and impulsively reached out to circle his forearm with her hand. She looked up at him, trembling with a desperate urgency to really make him *feel* her sincerity.

'There's no need for you to pour your heart out at…this hour…' Rafael's mouth felt dry. He cleared his throat.

'I want to,' Amy said earnestly.

Now both her small hands were resting on his folded arms and he knew that he was reacting like any man would when confronted by a sexy woman wearing nothing but an oversized dressing gown. Even if the sexy woman was not the sort he could ever really be attracted to. On any other level, he told himself, bar the physical.

'I *am* out of his league.' She tried to imagine James being thrown in with her family and failed. James was charming but fastidious. He would talk to anybody but he socialised with people who laughed at the same things he did and enjoyed the same lavish lifestyle that he had. Right now, he would be one of the lads with all the juniors, but once back in England he wouldn't dream of having any of them over to his house for dinner. It didn't make him a nasty person, just one who had grown up in a completely different world from the rest of them. 'I don't know how I could ever have thought that he might be interested in me. I met some of his friends…when I've catered for them at the office…and the women are nothing like me. They're all…*posh*…' She giggled sheepishly and launched into an imitation of a posh London socialite discussing the weather.

When she laughed like that, he noticed her robe slithered open just a fraction. He could definitely see the swell of her breasts and he nearly groaned aloud.

'Apology…accepted…'

He tried to shift back but, of course, pressed against the window ledge, he had zero room for manoeuvre. So he remained there, turned on, making sure she didn't get any closer, hoping she didn't look down. As horny as a teenager. Him! The man who controlled his enjoyments, who never found himself in the grip of wayward emotions!

'Thank you.' Amy meant it. From the bottom of her heart. Whatever emotions she happened to be feeling, she never stinted on it. And right now it happened to be regret.

She reached up, tiptoeing because he was so much taller than her, and closed her eyes. She meant to give him a peck on the cheek. Something warm, friendly and entirely *appropriate*.

Instead…

CHAPTER SEVEN

THE last woman Rafael had touched had been Elizabeth, and she was a tall, angular woman. In comparison, Amy was as slight and as fragile as a piece of bone china. He almost felt as though she would break if he was too rough.

Conflicting emotions rushed through him in a tidal wave. What the hell was he doing, pulling her into him? Kissing her as though his life depended on it? He couldn't get enough of those soft lips opening up to the pressure of his hungry, questing mouth. She whimpered and his tenuous grasp over his self-control slipped just a notch further. This was nothing like he had ever felt before. This *letting go* was exhilarating and terrifying at the same time.

He pulled away but it was hard, harder still to hold her at arm's length, watch her clutch the giant towelling robe around her as she glared at him, cheeks flushed, mouth still quivering from the impact of his.

He raked his fingers through his hair. 'That shouldn't have happened.'

Amy opened her mouth to tell him that he was damned right, that she hadn't come into his room to be *accosted* by him, that it would be no good trying to lay the blame at her door! Instead, she heard herself say, 'Why not?'

When, she thought frantically, was she *ever* going to be able to rely on her mouth to say the *right thing?* When?

'What I meant…' she rushed headlong into the first excuse that popped into her head '…was *why?* Yes…*why* did what happened…*happen*?'

'You're right,' Rafael murmured slowly. 'Why not?'

'That's not what I intended to say!'

'No.' He gave her a slow, bone-meltingly sexy smile. 'Truth has a nasty habit of ambushing us, hasn't it?' Any lingering doubts disappeared. Why had he been concerned? Why had he been trying to find answers to questions he had needlessly been asking himself? She had reduced the whole matter to two simple words; *why not?*

He wanted her, for reasons he couldn't begin to explain, and she wanted him. And they were both adults. And therefore *why not?*

'What you wanted to say is that you want me…'

Amy desperately wanted to disagree. She stared at him in mute, tortured silence as the hand that had gently pushed her away from him now began to lazily caress her arms.

'Don't even try to deny it,' Rafael continued into the unbroken silence. 'You make a very bad liar.' He stroked her hair and felt the fair, silky mass tangle around his fingers.

'I didn't come in here to…to…'

'Make a pass a me?' He let his finger slide along the smooth column of her neck, down to the V of the robe, which she had primly pulled tight around her. 'How am I to believe that when you come into my bedroom practically naked…?'

Amy was justifiably horrified. All she had to do now was scramble her horror into some healthy anger and storm out. Unfortunately his finger was doing all kinds of things to her nervous system. Sending it into mad, racing overdrive for starters.

'I'm not "practically naked"!' She drew the robe tighter around her. A nun couldn't be more heavily protected! However, she was excruciatingly aware of her nudity underneath, of her nipples rubbing against the coarse cotton, turning them into erect, sensitised peaks. 'And I didn't come here…'

'I know. If you were the sort of woman who came into my room to proposition me, with nothing on but a flimsy dressing gown, then I wouldn't be interested. But that wouldn't be *you,* would it?' He bent down and teased her parted mouth with his tongue. He could have had her there and then, his need was so overpowering, but he fought down the impulse to rush. He wanted to take this slowly, wanted to savour the taste of every bit of her.

'There's no need for you to apologise about…anything.' He caressed her neck as he continued to kiss her. He couldn't even break apart to talk so he murmured into her mouth.

Amy felt her bones turn to jelly. This was utter madness! Impulsive or not, she had never been so impulsive that she had hopped into bed with a man because *she fancied him.* There had always been a build-up. Dates, the gradual exploration of personalities, some sort of real friendship. This was in another league altogether. It was primitive, fast and brutal in the way it had caught her off guard. This was no delicate, gradual process. She didn't want him pulling away. She didn't even want him talking. She just wanted him to yank open her towelling robe and drag her onto the bed! What next? she wondered shakily. Would the ground suddenly start moving under her feet, as it did in soppy love songs when two people kissed?

In a daze, she was aware of him pulling her towards the bed. She was also aware that he was as fantastically turned on as she was. She felt faint. Against his boxers, his erection was huge.

Rafael leaned over her. Her fair hair spilled across the

pillow and she was still clutching that robe as if her life depended on it.

'There's still time for you to…change your mind.' He dredged up the last civilised bone in his body. 'The door's right there and I won't stop you if you decide you want to use it.'

Amy eyed it. 'I don't normally…do this sort of thing…'

'What sort of thing? The *men* sort of thing?'

'The jumping-into-bed-with-a-man-after-one-day sort of thing…'

'I knew we'd find something in common. I'm going to take my boxers off now. Think you want me to do that?'

Amy nodded as her vocal cords gave up on her.

She watched and gulped. She wasn't one to make comparisons but…

Rafael frowned. 'What's the matter?' If she was going to back out now! He doubted whether a cold shower would come anywhere close to doing the trick. He slid onto the bed next to her and turned her to face him.

'You're gripping that robe for dear life. Why? If you want me…'

'You're…*quite big,* aren't you?'

Rafael looked at her in frank astonishment. 'Six foot one. I wouldn't call myself a giant.'

'No. I mean…*down there…*'

The penny dropped and Rafael smiled slowly at her. 'And that scares you?' He gently eased her clenched fist from the robe and guided it down until she tentatively circled him with her fingers.

Yes, she thought wildly, but it was also impressive.

'Some simple biology,' he breathed unsteadily as her hand found its own rhythm and he was free to let his own hands wander, under the robe and along her waist, then upwards to her breast. At this point he had to cling to his self-control, especially as her rhythm was now quickening. 'A woman is built to accommodate a man, whatever his size. And you'll have to stop…doing what you're doing…' he put his hand over hers '…or else I won't be responsible for my body doing what comes naturally…'

His breathing steadied but it took a while and gave him a glimpse of a forgotten world. The world in which passion ruled intellect and sex was purely pleasurable rather than an essentially well-mannered meeting of bodies. How long had it been since he had had to fight not to lose control?

He pushed her onto her back and pinned her hands against the pillow so that he could straddle her. The robe had dropped open, revealing the perfection of her breasts.

Rafael drew his breath in swiftly. Her big, rosy nipples begged for his attention. With deliberate slowness, he peeled the robe back further.

Amy squirmed in eager anticipation. Rafael was holding her down, but she felt faint with excitement. She almost didn't want him to let her go, but then if he hadn't, how could he do what he was doing now? Kissing her neck until she quivered? Moving slowly down so that he could begin to suckle on her nipple, which was such an agonisingly pleasurable sensation that Amy could only gasp and wriggle against his determined mouth.

He slid his hands under her waist so that she was arched even more up towards him, a willing offering for him to take.

With feverish excitement, Amy wound her fingers through his hair. Instead of closing her eyes, she looked down at him as he explored her breasts with his mouth and tongue, watched with mounting heat as his dark head moved between them, pleasuring first one then the other.

She tried to push herself up so that she could touch him as well, but he was having none of it. He just wouldn't let her.

His tongue trailing across her stomach made her groan

aloud and she *did* close her eyes as his hands moved to slide under her bottom, levering her up so that he could nuzzle the soft hair between her legs.

She moaned and then sucked in her breath sharply because now he was no longer nuzzling but exploring her with his tongue and mouth.

To open her eyes and look at him moving on her would have been too unbearably erotic.

But when his questing tongue continued flicking against her over-sensitised nub, she had to reach down and tug him gently away or else risk her own early and unwanted orgasm!

'Not yet,' was all she could manage to croak.

She wanted to touch him too. Had to! Had to lick his flat brown nipples, then do her own tactile exploration of his magnificent body. He was amazingly well muscled. Not surprising given his profession, but it was still a heady turn-on to contour the flat, hard planes of his stomach with her hand.

Then she pleasured him as he had her, making it slow and leisurely.

They both knew when the moment was right. Never before had Rafael felt so in tune with someone else's body. It was almost as if she could communicate to him through her senses.

He entered her the good, old-fashioned way. Time enough for a more adventurous approach. Right now…right now Rafael just needed her too much.

He was carried away by his body's driving needs and no longer in charge of the steering wheel. It was only afterwards as they were lying next to one another that a sudden thought occurred to Rafael.

'We didn't use any protection.'

Amy had to make an effort to join in with his perfectly serious, sensible line of conversation. All she wanted to do was enjoy this wonderful feeling of perfect contentment and play with his hair. Just as she was doing at the moment. Reluctantly, she propped herself up on her elbows and looked at him.

'No,' she agreed. 'We didn't. I guess…things just happened too quickly. One minute I was standing at your door with my ready-made apology, the next minute we were somehow in bed together. Not much in-depth chat in between.'

'Which could be a problem.'

'Well, what if I told you that I wasn't protected?'

Amy didn't know what she had expected in response to this provocative remark, but she hadn't expected the complete stillness, the closed, shuttered expression.

'It's no joking matter, Amy. Are you or aren't you?'

She pulled back, suddenly disturbed by his response, then she told herself shakily that of course she was being paranoid. 'Of course I'm protected,' she told him truthfully. 'You needn't worry that I'm going to show up on your doorstep in a year's time with an unexpected present in a basket. I'm not that irresponsible!'

'No. Old habits die hard,' Rafael said, also truthfully. 'Making sure a woman has no agenda is just something I've become accustomed to doing over the years…'

'What kind of agenda would a woman have…?' *With you?* she nearly added, having more or less made her mind up that Rafael's staggering sexual self-assurance was due to the fact that he had affairs with the rich and possibly famous who stayed at the house. Well, it wasn't as though they would be looking to him as a meal ticket, was it?

'The usual kind.' Rafael shrugged.

'You're a commitment phobe…' Amy said slowly. She didn't know why it hurt to think that he was laying down warnings about getting involved with him, considering there was no chance of that as she was going to be returning to England within days.

And even if she *had* been staying on, even if she had been spending the rest of her life living next to him, did she really imagine that he would be contemplating marriage and kids on the first night they had slept together?

They hadn't even been on a date together! At least, not really. Taking someone out because you felt sorry for them didn't count as a date and sleeping with someone because there happened to be a spark of mutual physical attraction didn't count as love.

She wondered where that word had come from and frowned.

'I wouldn't say I'm phobic about the matter,' Rafael inserted. 'Why are you looking so worried? Being careful is part of my nature.'

'Am I looking worried?' Amy laughed blithely. 'Does that sound like a worried laugh to you?' There, that was more like it! She was here, they had just made fabulous love and every part of her just wanted to carry on enjoying the man next to her while she could.

'Did I hurt you?'

'Hurt me? How?'

'By wanting to be sure that contraception was in place.'

'No. No, you didn't. And why should you have?' Amy looked at him seriously. 'I would be worried sick if we had had sex without protection. Men always seem to think that they're the ones who would be put out if a woman they slept with became pregnant. They never stop to think that the woman would probably be in a much more difficult situation! Do you ask *all* the women you sleep with if they're on the pill?'

'No, because I generally take the matter in hand myself.' Rafael was beginning to wonder how the conversation had managed to become so prolonged. As always, she was running away with it and somehow dragging him behind her in her wake.

'What do you mean?'

'What do you think I mean?' He leant forward to kiss her mouth and she wriggled away so that she could give him a stern look.

'Okay. I get the picture. But why are you so afraid of commitment?'

Rafael groaned. 'Are we going to spend the rest of the night talking?' he asked. 'Because I can think of better things to do.' He gave her a hot, brooding look that sent her pulses racing.

'Like what?' Amy asked innocently, moving fractionally closer to him so that she could rub her body against his.

'I think you know…'

She did and this time they made love languorously, exploring each other's bodies as the hands on the clock ticked past, rolling night into day and finally, completely sated, they fell asleep wrapped around each other.

Amy woke to find an empty space where Rafael should have been. Immediately she thought about their commitment conversation, which had been abandoned in the haze of making love. She wondered whether he had got cold feet and disappeared back to the safety of his gardener's cottage.

But he hadn't.

He strolled in, wearing nothing but his boxer shorts and carrying a tray on which were bagels, jams and cups of frothy cappuccino that he had bought from the nearest café.

'You should have woken me up!' Amy squirmed into a sitting position and Rafael watched as her very delectable breasts peeped over the top of the duvet cover. On cue, he hardened in immediate response.

'You looked too peaceful.' He deposited the tray on the bed next to her and sat down. 'Now, before we eat anything…' He snapped open the lid of the small glass jar of jam and dipped his finger in, then he proceeded to coat her nipples with jam while Amy giggled, only catching her breath as he began to suck off the sticky, sweet stuff. He did a very thorough job, licking until her nipples were shiny and everywhere inside her was melting and wanting more of the same attention.

'There,' Rafael said. Then he laughed when she adopted a pleading voice and said, with wrenching femininity, 'Please, sir, can I have some more…?'

'I think that can be arranged in a minute. For now. Coffee. Bagels. We New Yorkans are very good at bagels. We make the best in the world.' He tore off a piece and fed it to her. This felt like a holiday to him. He had made a couple of work-related calls on the way to the corner shop and had checked his emails first thing before she had awakened, but aside from that work had disappeared off the radar. And here he was, feeding bread to a woman in what any impartial outsider might have labelled a *romantic gesture*. Except romance had never been his thing. A night spent with a woman would always involve him leaving at the crack of dawn for work, after bestowing the perfunctory kiss on the cheek to his sleeping partner, if indeed she was still asleep. Usually, like him, she would have been up and raring to go as well. And if it had been a weekend, he might have got up at a more lei-surely time, but the new day would have seen him in front of the newspaper, checking on the stock markets, having grabbed a quick bite with his partner. And the quick bite would *never* have been in bed!

'Oh, any old good bread shop can sell a bagel that's not half bad,' Amy teased, personally thinking that she had yet to taste anything quite so delicious in her life, 'and any old person can go along and buy it. The test of the real man is whether he can rustle one up himself!'

'Oh. You mean real men bake bread!'

'Exactly!' Oh, but this was bliss! The banter. The easy

camaraderie. Just this weird feeling that she could trust this man to the ends of the earth.

Not that she would get the chance, given that she was leaving the country in the blink of an eye.

'Well, that sorts out my nagging doubts about my gender,' Rafael returned without skipping a beat. 'I'm a mouse.'

Amy laughed and marvelled that someone could be so tuned in to her quirky sense of humour! And later on, she marvelled that a man could have such physical stamina and then, close on the heels of that thought, that he could arouse her so quickly, so thoroughly and so *often* that she just couldn't seem to get enough of him!

Of course, she cautioned herself the following day, as they explored more nooks and crannies along the coast, this was just a holiday romance. In fact, not even a romance *as such*. More of a fling. A fling without guilt or conscience.

In fact, as they enjoyed dinner *her way,* which meant jeans for him at a busy pizza bar that served the biggest pizzas she had ever seen, she told herself *firmly* that it was just as well their little dalliance was destined to be short-lived because it helpfully removed all those silly happy-ever-after romantic notions.

She could enjoy his company without looking for more. Looking for more was boring, she decided. The harder you looked for a future, the greater the chance that you were missing out on the present. And the present, two days later, was another trip to Manhattan, which was even more fantastic than the first because this time they were lovers. No arguments, no bristling, just the corny business of holding hands and thirstily fishing for information. And yet again he had managed to nab James's company apartment, which was very handy to say the least.

It was only as her departure day became more than just round the corner that certain frightening home truths began to creep beneath her convenient layer of self-assurances.

The first self-assurance to go was that what she felt was only skin deep. It wasn't.

The second was that leaving would be a blessing because it would eliminate pointless dreams. It wasn't and it didn't.

And then there was the small matter of just *enjoying the moment.* As her penultimate day drew to a close, she found that she just couldn't enjoy the moment when she knew full well that there were no more moments to come.

She had been fed on a diet of *amazing* and now, as she stared down the road to a future of mediocres, she realised that she was greedy. She wanted more.

He had cooked for her. At his house. Nothing fancy but she got the feeling that it was something he seldom did, which made it special. It also made her wonder whether there might just be a slim chance that she actually meant something to him.

It hadn't escaped her notice as the days had passed by that he had never, not once, not even in the heat of the moment when men, supposedly, said all sorts of rash things, talked about a future for them. She wasn't asking him to bring out his diary and fix a date for two month's time. She wasn't asking him to start selling off his valuables so that he could spend the money on flights across the Atlantic. On the other hand he had not once mentioned even the slightest possibility that one day he might just decide to visit London.

Even after she had exhaustively dangled all the wonderful things there were for him to see there, all the fabulous places to visit. All the historical sights, some of which she fabricated as her knowledge of history was a little thin.

'Don't you ever…hmm…' Amy aimed for the casual approach '…have the urge to leave this place?'

'This place being…' Rafael knew where the conversation was leading. Well, sooner or later it was going to happen because, however different she was from the women he had known, she wasn't so different that she would be immune to the same desire to build a relationship.

And the conversation was surely bound to happen at a moment like this, when they had finished making love and were enjoying the pleasurable warmth of its aftermath. He shifted so that he could look at her and she curved round so that she could remain lying in the crook of his arm while being able to see his face. She wanted to search it for clues although she was pretty sure she would find none there.

'This house. I mean, it's a very nice house, but still...don't you ever want to go gardening *somewhere else?* The world is full of big, *challenging* gardens, after all.'

'This is a very big garden.'

'I know it's *big*, Rafael, but you must know it like the back of your hand. The trees, the plants, the rose bushes...'

'You seem obsessed with rose bushes.' He nuzzled her hair, which smelt of shampoo and sun. It had to be said that she was a funny little thing. It was incredibly easy to tease her. Why? He supposed because she was so lacking in gravitas. He guiltily had to admit that there was something refreshing about her easygoing nature. But no, he told himself, she was a novelty and novelties wore off. The women he needed and wanted were the Elizabeths of this world, as fiercely competitive as he was, as understanding of his mammoth working hours as he was of theirs, as deeply interested in the stock markets as he was. And anyway, he uneasily reminded himself that he had only involved himself with the woman because she posed a possible threat to James, of whom he was very protective.

He vaguely recalled some plan or other to lull her away from any ideas she might have had of rekindling her interest in his brother once they had returned to the normality of England. Now, as she gazed at him, he resurrected all those healthy thoughts.

Because there was no way he had any intention of leading her up any garden paths.

He had taken time off, had deviated from his usual routine and, yes, he had enjoyed it, but it was time for him to get his normal, ordered, high-octane life back.

Communicating with his office via e-mail and phone calls was fine but it had to stop. As did their pleasant but passing little fling.

'Don't you yearn to…see the world?'

'I might if I didn't think that the familiar is as important as the unknown.'

'You're doing this deliberately, aren't you?'

'Doing what?' He inserted his thigh between hers and slowly moved it back and forth. She inhaled sharply and half closed her eyes.

'No. Don't.' Amy untangled herself from his erotic caress and firmly placed *her* leg over his. 'I want to talk, Rafael. And I don't want you confusing me. You're clever with your words but I don't want clever, I want *honest*. Do you realise that I leave tomorrow? This is the last night we're going to spend together and…' she breathed in deeply and said in one fast rush '…I *promised* myself that I wasn't to ask you any of this, but here goes…what's going to happen to us? I'm not asking for commitment from you, Rafael, but do we have any kind of short, very short, future? Obviously, you've got responsibilities here…those rose bushes….' She tried her hand at a weak joke but she could already sense him pulling back.

'Okay. Forget I said anything,' she whispered, wriggling away from him.

'No.' Rafael sighed and then did the one thing that brought home to her, like a hammer blow, just how ridiculous she had been to have started having those crazy things called hopes and dreams.

He got out of bed.

'We've had a good time over the past few days and you want to talk, then talk we shall. But I don't think bed is the best place for the conversation.'

'I don't want to talk,' Amy said miserably.

He didn't answer. He started getting dressed. Just his dressing gown, but it might as well have been a suit for the distance it suddenly placed between them.

Amy scrambled to do the same. It helped that he had disappeared into the bathroom, that place that had seen many a shared shower. She hurriedly slipped on her clothes and was fully dressed by the time he returned.

'Coffee?' he asked.

It's over, she heard. 'Okay.'

She watched in silence as he made them both a mug of coffee. Just in the space of a few days, she seemed to have become familiar with all his mannerisms, the way he lounged against the kitchen counter when he was waiting for the kettle to boil, the way he frowned and raked his fingers through his hair just before he said something he considered important, the way he rubbed the back of his neck when he was tired. It was a horrifying realisation because it showed just how much he had got under her skin.

'You want to know where this is going. That's what all these "don't you long to travel and see the world?" questions are leading.' She had sat at the kitchen table and Rafael now swivelled his chair and straddled it so that he was directly facing her. She could see that look on his face, that I'm-about-to-let-you-down-gently look. Poor Amy. Time for the Good-bye Talk.

'Oh, for goodness' sake, Rafael. There's no need to make such a song and dance about it!' She was going to work her way quickly through the coffee, while giving a speech of her own. 'I wasn't trying to arrange a date for you to come to England!'

'No? Then what about the short, short future?'

'Oh.' Amy shrugged. 'I guess it's what anyone would say in my shoes. It doesn't mean I'm hearing wedding bells. I mean, it's been a laugh but, as we established from day one, we're not soul mates, are we?' She laughed to emphasise the silliness of such a notion. 'But, hey, I just thought we could keep in touch by e-mail…you could come over some time if you ever had a craving to visit Kew Gardens and see how we English do the gardening scene. To be honest,' she felt emboldened to continue, 'I was just being polite. I didn't intend to spark off an international incident. But as we know, you take life way too seriously so I should have known how you would react!'

Rafael didn't say anything. She had pre-empted what he had intended to say. And that was good. They understood one another. There would be no need for him to wrench her off him when the time came to part. Good! Couldn't be better.

He surfaced to realise that she was fidgeting, saying something about leaving.

'Already?' His eyebrows shot up in surprise as their last night became rapidly condensed into their last few minutes. A groundswell of *something* seemed to gather apace inside him and he quickly buried it.

'It's late, Rafael.'

'Would you have stayed if I had decided that we did have some sort of short, short future?'

'I haven't finished my packing. And I'd really like to get back for at least part of the last night's festivities. James is planning on fireworks.'

'You could watch them here.'

It was tempting. Sitting outside with him, arms around each other. Tempting but pointless. She needed to get away as fast as she could.

'I could but I'm not going to.' She sighed and moved towards him, just one last hug, just something for her box of memories. She placed her arms around him. In her flats, she only reached the top of his shoulder. He buried his head in her hair and squeezed her. To his horror, he wanted to beg her not to go, to stay the night. Very gently he pushed her away and firmly reined in his galloping thoughts.

'That's fine.'

The back of her throat began to ache from the effort of holding back the tears.

'I'll drop you.'

'No! Please don't. I…' She turned away and began walking towards the front door. 'I know the way back to the house. I know all the short cuts! And the fresh air would be nice.' She reached for the door knob and gave him one last glance. 'Been fun, Rafael. Take care of those rose bushes. You know I'm obsessed by them.'

Rafael was seriously beginning to regret that he hadn't made agreeable noises about the short, short future she had mentioned. But it was too late now. He couldn't retrieve the situation without sounding weak. He watched her look around to see if she was forgetting anything, then he watched as she walked out of the door and out of his life for good.

Mission accomplished, he told himself. There was no way she would ever look twice at James again. He knew her well enough by now to know that she would be as honest with herself as she possibly could and that honesty would force her to admit that, on the back of what they had enjoyed, anything she might have felt for James would have been an illusion.

Along the way he had had a very nice time. What more could he ask for?

CHAPTER EIGHT

AMY had never been backward at learning lessons. From Freddie, she had learnt to avoid men who placed personal ambition over everything and everyone. Men like that viewed other people as stepping-stones, women included. And from James, her unavailable crush, she had learnt that rich men liked women who melded into their lifestyles. They didn't want the challenge of a woman who thought holidays every three weeks were a waste of time after a while or whose social consciences were pricked by the extravagance of people who had houses scattered across the globe, half of which they never got around to visiting.

She knew that because she had ended up spending the flight back to London next to him. It had been the first time she had spent more than ten minutes conversing with him. He had been as sweet and charming as she had expected, asking her all the right things, trying his best to get her to reveal how exactly she had spent her time in the Hamptons, because he hadn't seen much of her at the organised social events.

Amy had valiantly avoided mentioning Rafael. Okay, so it wasn't as though it would have made any difference, but it had still felt like an invasion of her privacy. She hadn't want to share those moments with anyone else, least of all James. She hadn't known how he would react to the fact that his gardener had had a fling with a guest and she hadn't been about to be responsible for anyone getting fired.

In the face of her stubborn vagueness, he had eventually dropped his questioning, and Amy had had no trouble in getting him to talk about himself. James enjoyed talking about himself and he was very good at it. He involved his listener. In fact, it was easy to forget that ninety per cent of the conversation, if you analysed it, was about him. What he did, the places he had been, the sights he had seen and of course what he thought about…well, just about everything. Reading between the lines hadn't required too much effort. At the end of seven hours or so, Amy had had a pretty clear idea of what made James tick and it wasn't a driving curiosity to discover what lay outside the confines of his own gilded life.

Rafael had been spot on when he had told her that she was out of James's league, although she rather thought that they just didn't share the same space at all.

Unlike she and Rafael…

Amy had perfected a technique when it came to thinking about Rafael. She avoided it by immediately thinking about something else. She was pretty sure it was beginning to work.

Now, she thought about how far she had come in the space of two months. Two long months during which she had paid attention to what her experiences had taught her and changed her life accordingly.

The first thing she had done was to quit working for James. Not because she didn't want to see him. Quite frankly, she didn't care much one way or the other. What she didn't want was to be reminded of Rafael and James was a link to Rafael. She didn't trust herself not to ask him, casually, in passing, how that gardener of his was doing. Her pride would never have recovered if she were to be tempted down that road because one thing she had realised pretty quickly was that she had meant nothing to Rafael. He had had no intention of pursuing their relationship. Amy told herself that the Atlantic Ocean was a pretty big obstacle anyway, and he had probably been astute enough to realise that from the word go, but in her heart she knew that he could have made a meaningless promise to keep in touch.

When she thought back to the way she had asked him about a *future*, she cringed in embarrassment.

She told herself that it should be easy to forget him because of the way he had casually dismissed her after the most wonderful few days of her life, but her heart struggled to listen to her head.

The radical change of lifestyle had helped, though.

Not only had she quit James's company but she had gone back to college to specialise. She would never have Freddie's pie-in-the-sky dreams about becoming a celebrity chef, but that didn't mean that she should remain stuck in a groove, doing low-key catering for companies when she knew she could achieve more.

A healthy new start, she told herself.

Her mum was helping her out with the finances and she was filling the gaps by doing the occasional spot of catering for friends of friends of friends, people who were happy enough to allow her to try out some of her experimental dishes on them.

So she wasn't too surprised when she got a call from a woman, to whom she had been recommended, asking whether she could do something on the weekend for her boss who was having a little private gathering at his house in London.

'He's not often over,' she said, 'and you'll be paid well if you agree to the job.' She named a figure that made Amy gasp.

'Well…I suppose so…address?'

'And the name…?'

'Lee. Mr Lee.'

But not James, of course. He would have called himself had he wanted her services, which he had, once, since she had left to do her own thing, and professional discretion prohibited her from asking for more details.

She took the details, was pleased to be told that she could broadly cook what she wanted, and promptly forgot the co-incidence of the name until, five days later, she was standing in front of an immensely expensive-looking Georgian town house. Claire, still working at James's company, had offered to help her set up but Amy had refused. It was a tiny meal, just four people, something she could manage on her own with her eyes closed.

She didn't like going to a new place on her own, but neither did she want Claire's chatterbox company. She felt whacked.

She rang the doorbell and was inspecting her bags of goodies, doing a mental checklist to make sure nothing had been forgotten, when the door was answered. She didn't look up. At least not immediately. She was too busy zipping up the cool bag that contained the cold ingredients that she would need for the pudding.

So the first things she saw were the shoes. Tan brogues. Very shiny. Very well made. Very expensive. In fact, very what you would expect to find standing on the doorstep of an immaculate Georgian house in one of the best post codes in London.

Amy stood up smartly. Expensive people, she had found, had very short temper spans. They paid their money and expected their exquisite food to magically appear on their table. Witnessing any of the less than magical clutter that went into the preparation of the exquisite food was not some-thing they enjoyed. Nor did they like too much involvement with the people stirring the pots behind the scenes.

The apology was already on her lips. In fact, her hand was

reaching out in introduction when recognition slammed into shock and she felt herself stagger backwards. She had to blink because she was so sure that her mind was playing tricks on her.

He couldn't be there! Standing in front of her! Standing on the steps of a house that would have cost millions!

'Hi, Amy. Guess you thought we were never going to meet again?'

'Rafael?'

'Come on in. You look as though you're about to faint on the pavement.'

She was dimly aware of him bringing in everything she had been carrying with her, leading her through a magnificent entrance hallway with shining black and white flagstones, through to the kitchen, which was sumptuous, a miracle of high-tech equipment. The sort of kitchen most caterers dreamed of one day owning.

She felt as though her head had suddenly been stuffed with cotton wool.

'You probably want to know what the hell is going on…' Rafael deposited her into one of the chairs by the kitchen table. It was leather. Black leather to match the granite work surfaces and the gleaming, matching table top. Everything gleamed through lack of use.

'What the hell is going on?' Amy obliged.

'Do you want something to drink?'

'No! I want to know what's going on!' She couldn't help it. Her heart was beginning to pound. She had remembered every inch of him, but she had somehow forgotten his impact. 'I was told…the woman said…you were a *Mr Lee*…I thought…'

'James is my brother. I used his surname so you wouldn't know you were cooking for me.'

'What?' Amy's head shot up and she looked at Rafael in stunned bewilderment. 'What are you talking about?'

The past two months had not been good for Rafael. He had dismissed his liaison with her as a pleasant but passing interlude, something that had sprung up on the back of his breakup from Elizabeth. But the memory of her had lingered in his head like a burr until every area of his life had been subtly but glaringly compromised. He had found himself staring through windows when he should have been staring at his computer, thinking of her when his head should have been full of reports and deal-making. He had had to stifle the urge to phone his brother and ask what she was doing until he hadn't been able to stop himself any longer. At which point he had learnt that she had left the company and in those few split seconds when he had realised that he might not see her again Rafael had made his mind up.

There had been nothing stopping him from coming to England. He had a house there and he ran the company, for God's sake, even if he had decided a long time ago to focus his energies in New York.

He hadn't had to give reasons to anyone. He had known, without a shadow of smugness, that he was the head guy and everyone else would make way for him, as they had.

And he hadn't questioned his compelling motives for seeking her out. In his head, the reason was simple. The relationship, fling, affair, call it what you will, had not yet run its course and there was nothing more inconvenient than unfinished business.

He had begun something that needed to be closed and he was pretty sure that she would feel the same way as he did.

However, he had not fully envisaged the reaction he would get from her, but it was dawning on him that joy and elation weren't heavily featured.

'My *half*-brother, I should say.'

'But you're *his gardener*…' Amy spluttered, bewildered.

'What I know about gardens would fit on the back of a postage stamp,' Rafael admitted.

'You mean you *lied to me*?'

Rafael flushed.

'Why? *Why?* Why would you *do* that?'

'If you calm down and let me get a word in edgewise, then I might be able to explain.'

'You want me to *calm down*? I don't *feel calm*! You lied to me and now here you are…*for what*?'

Rafael pushed himself away from the counter and reached inside one of the cupboards for a couple of glasses, into which he poured them both a measure of brandy. 'Drink.'

'I don't want a drink! I want to know what you're doing here! And why you lied to me! And please don't give me any speeches about hating hysterical women. I feel hysterical!'

But she took the glass from him with trembling hands and swallowed a few mouthfuls, which instantly calmed her down.

He had pulled up a chair and was sitting facing her. Amy felt faint. 'You can't be James's brother. You look nothing like him.'

'*Half*-brother.' Rafael sighed. 'We share a mother but my father was Spanish, hence my colouring.'

'I don't understand. Why were you pretending to be a gardener?'

'Long story but…' He explained. If he had expected dawning comprehension followed by nodding acceptance he was sorely mistaken. The dawning comprehension was there, sure enough, but it was accompanied by a look of slowly spreading horror.

'So…' Amy had now finished the glass of brandy. Just like his identity, she assumed his request for a caterer had been as bogus as a three pound note. She had lain in bed night after night fantasising about this man, spinning dreams in which he ended up declaring his undying love after which they would spend the rest of their fairy-tale lives building up a thriving garden centre in the countryside. She felt a ball of resentment well up inside her that he had taken her for a ride, made a fool of her. She wondered whether he and James had laughed about her behind her back.

'Let me get this straight. You were asked to spy on your brother—'

'Keep an eye on...and half-brother.'

'And in the process you met me and thought that you would pretend to be someone you weren't...because...now why would you do that?' Revelation struck her with the force of a sledgehammer.

'I told you about James, didn't I?'

'Don't start leap-frogging to any conclusions—'

'I happened to mention James—in fact, if I recall correctly, poured my heart out and confessed that I had a crush on the boss, on *your brother*!'

Rafael's teeth snapped together in frustration as he followed the train of her thoughts and watched them gather momentum.

'Is that when you decided that it might be a good idea not to disclose your identity?' She correctly interpreted his silence for validation of what she was saying.

She had thought that nothing could hurt as much as leaving him behind. She had been wrong. It hurt much, much more to realise that she had been used.

'I'm right, aren't I?' she said quietly. 'You figured you could pump me for information if you pretended to be the lowly gardener. After all, the lowly caterer would be far more likely to confide in someone of equal standing.'

'Of course I was interested when you told me how you felt about James. Do you think it would have been natural if I hadn't been?'

'Too interested to tell me that you were his brother—oh, sorry, his *half*-brother, not that that makes a bit of difference!'

Amy had thought that she could remember every word that had passed between them, but now she was trying to she found that she couldn't, not quite. Snippets of conversation came and went in her head. 'No wonder you knew so much about James. No wonder you felt free to tell me that I was *out of his league.*'

'I told you that to try and make you see sense. James…is predictable in his choice of women.'

'Oh…so you were *protecting* me!'

Rafael ran his fingers through his hair and scowled. This was the woman who had been wreaking havoc with his carefully ordered life, ruining his concentration, sending him into a mental tailspin. He had done the unthinkable and come to London *in pursuit* and what did he find? A shrieking harridan who wasn't prepared to hear him out!

The shrieking harridan was now proceeding to give him the full, unexpurgated benefit of her mind.

'Oh, I *don't think so!* You thought I might have been after his money, didn't you? You thought it might be a good idea to sound me out, find out what my game was… It's all falling into place now.'

In the midst of her rant, which had sent the colour rushing to her face, Rafael still couldn't control the way his eyes compulsively fastened on her, the way he wanted to shut her up by kissing her. He stood up abruptly so that he could pour himself another drink. Not brandy. Nothing that went to his brain like a match. Wine. A glass of red wine.

He poured himself his glass of wine and stood leaning against the counter. He didn't expect her to storm over to him. Nor did he think that she would have the nerve to snatch the glass from him and tip the contents down the sink while telling him that, uh-uh, there was no way he was going to ignore what she had to say by getting drunk.

Then she stood in front of him, hands on hips, daring him to challenge her.

Rafael, who had absolutely no experience of a woman enraged, instinctively knew better than to rise to the challenge.

'Now I know why you were so horrible to me to start with. You're *a horrible person*! Until you decided that you would be better off being just a little bit nicer…because if you want information, being horrible isn't really the best way to get it, is it!'

'I was horrible because I had to rescue you from a tree in the middle of the night,' Rafael pointed out reasonably.

'And then all those times when I caught you in front of a computer… Do you know, I actually *believed* you when you said you were just catching up on personal e-mails?' She laughed incredulously at her own stupidity. 'Let's see… running an empire…catching up on personal e-mails… hmm…not much difference, is there?'

'Oh, for God's sake…' He glared at her in mounting frustration. 'Let's sit down and discuss this like adults—'

'Oh, I forgot!' Amy plastered a sickly, saccharine smile on her face. 'You *hate* women who express themselves in any voice louder than half a decibel! It's just not *adult* or *civilised* to rant and rave even when you've found out that the man you…' for a moment she nearly said the word *love* and was furious with herself for the near miss '…had a fling with was using you all along to try and extract information! Well, you know something, Rafael? I'm not very adult and I'm not very civilised when it comes to things like that!' She turned her back and began gathering up all her assorted bags with utensils and ingredients for a meal she had never been destined to prepare anyway.

'And you could have spared me a taxi fare tonight,' she yelled shakily, 'dragging all this stuff here for no reason!' She stared down at her feet, drained.

'Okay. I made a mistake.'

Amy ignored him. She had managed to gather all her belongings together and was now struggling with them to the door. She had ingredients for a delicious meal for four. Most of the dishes had been pre-prepared, with only the finishing touches left to do, but it still meant a lot of stuff to carry. She tried not to think about the effort of dragging it all along the road, bag-lady style, while she frantically stopped every five paces so that she could try and flag down a taxi, because there was no way she could manage the trip back to her house on public transport.

'I'm not interested in hearing what you have to say,' she told him coldly, because she had to say something. He was standing in front of her, blocking her way out. She just couldn't look at him because it was like looking at a stranger.

'I'll drop you back to your house, if that's what you want, and we can talk on the way.'

'I told you…I'm not interested. I'm through talking. I only wish I'd never set eyes on you in the first place.'

'You don't mean that,' Rafael muttered huskily.

What had he expected? He was realising that he really didn't know. A bit of discomfort, yes. Because there was no way that he could have skirted round the truth. He couldn't have shown up in his role of pretend gardener, somehow mysteriously passing through, and he hadn't wanted to. The truth was unavoidable and, yes, he had known that she would have been surprised, shocked even. But her series of questions, her rapid deductions that had gathered pace before his eyes, had made it difficult for him to object. Not that there was a great deal to object to. Somehow she had managed to find little snippets of truth and string them together into a portrait of himself that he barely recognised.

And now she was talking of leaving!

He was driven by a crazy impulse to snatch the bags off her and lock her in the house until they had sorted things out between them. Which, he knew, meant until they ended up in bed together.

'Do you mind getting out of my way?'

Rafael realised that she was no longer yelling. Her voice was flat and distant and in some way that was far worse.

'Yes. I mind.'

'Then I guess we'll just have to stay here until you decide to move, but I won't be having any post-mortem conversation with you.' She sat down on top of the holdall in which the majority of the food had been transported. She cupped her chin on her balled fist and stared somewhere in the region of his calves.

After the first furious volley of hurt and outrage, her mind seemed to have zoned out totally.

She thought back to their brief time together, lethargically piecing together strands of his behaviour that now made sense in retrospect. Like the way he had persuaded her not to say anything to anyone about his presence on the grounds. She hadn't questioned it at the time, but, really and truly, why on earth should a gardener be so secretive? Then there had been his lack of interest in all things *green*. She had talked at length about her work, about her love of cooking, about her favourite dishes. He had skirted over all mention of gardens and landscaping and flowers and plants and horticulture in general, with a dismissive shrug of his broad shoulders.

Then there had been the small matter of the apartment, so-called company apartment, in its prime location in Manhattan. And his fantastic car. The list was endless and Amy could have kicked herself for not paying a single scrap of attention to any of the warning signs that had been flashing in front of her in bold neon lettering.

In the middle of her clamouring thoughts, she realised that he had stooped down so that he was now on her level, looking at her squarely in the face and way too close to her for her liking.

Amy stared at him blankly.

'I was wrong,' Rafael told her grimly. 'And you're going to listen to what I have to say whether you like it or not. And I don't intend conversing to you squatting on the floor.' He stood up and yanked her to her feet and Amy toppled against him and pulled back in dismay.

She opened her mouth to repeat her mantra about having nothing further to say to him, but she didn't get very far before she was being swept off her feet and carried—*carried!*—over his shoulder, out of the kitchen and into the sitting room where she was unceremoniously placed on the sofa.

Rafael could no more believe he had done that than she could.

He briefly contemplated locking the door and pocketing the key but every civilised instinct in him reared up at that extreme.

Instead, he went across to the sofa. She had scooted up one end and was watching him warily.

'I should have told you who I was from the beginning but I didn't because I honestly didn't want my time interrupted. I might not be known to the English crew, but everyone else would know exactly who I was and would be damned curious to find out why I was skulking in the grounds. My mother asked me to be there and I did what she wanted.'

'But then even if you *had* been tempted to tell me who I really were, you soon wised up to the fact that you would find out a lot more about me and my motives if you kept quiet.'

'Correct.' He looked away and relaxed back into the chair, stretching out his long legs in front of him and clasping his hands behind his head. 'I wanted to find out for myself if you were after James for a reason.' He shifted so that he was looking at her now. She had come prepared for a night of hard work, had tied her hair ferociously back into two plaits, was wearing the plainest of clothes. But she still looked edible. In fact, just as he had remembered her.

'By the time we made love, I knew that you weren't interested in James and, if you had been, his money had had nothing to do with anything.'

Amy felt hot and shaky. He was certainly respecting her space, was making sure to keep a healthy distance between them, but his eyes were boring holes through her. She didn't like it when he referred to them making love. It was easier to concentrate on his deception and feel angry about it when she wasn't thinking of him as a man, as her lover.

'Does that make you react?' Rafael asked softly. His posture was relaxed but his gaze, fixed on her flushed face, was intent and watchful.

'What? I don't know what you're talking about.'

'Oh, yes, you do. The memory of us…in bed…don't you want to know why I've come over to London?'

'No. And I don't care.'

'I couldn't get you out of my head,' Rafael confessed.

Amy snorted. 'You mean after you dismissed me without a backward glance?' She had an embarrassing recollection of asking him, on her point of departure, whether they might try and prolong their relationship. Remembered just as clearly his immediate, negative response.

'I wasn't on the lookout for a relationship with someone from this country.' He thought of Elizabeth. 'Or any country, for that matter,' he added.

'Oh, stop pretending, Rafael. You weren't on the lookout for a relationship with *me*. Do you remember telling me that I was out of James's league? Well, face it, you could have added your name to the category.' She heard the hard edge in her voice with dismay. Never before had she been bitter. She just wasn't a bitter person. At least, not until now.

She badly wanted to talk to someone in her family. One of her sisters. Or brothers.

She needed a familiar voice to tell her that she was going to be just fine.

'You were out of his league because James only looks at a certain type of woman. Call it lack of imagination on his part.'

'And you were imaginative enough to seduce me even though I wasn't your type.'

Too much talking. That had been the problem. Conversation with past girlfriends had been skin deep and work related. It seemed that he had done way too much talking with Amy. Had he really told her that she wasn't his type? Unfortunately it sounded horribly probable. One of those passing remarks to establish that he wasn't in the market for commitment. And she had listened and filed away the remark for future reference. She was a very good listener, he realised belatedly. He wondered what else might be brought up in evidence of his exploitative, horrible character.

'Obviously I don't…' Rafael, caught fully on the back foot for the first time in his life, was literally stuck for words. He scowled and stood up so that he could prowl the room. He needed movement.

'Don't what?'

'Don't date women who are clones of one another.' Well, actually, he did.

'I don't believe you. I think…do you know what I think?'

'I think we should put the past behind us and focus on the now. The now that brought me over here. Because you've been on my mind night and day since you left. Do you think I would have come over if you hadn't been? Do you think I would have put myself through *this* if I hadn't realised how much I still want you?'

Interrupted in mid-sentence, Amy could only stare at him. Yes, he wanted her and want was a very powerful thing, but what she heard wasn't a man who was open to the possibility of a relationship. What she heard was a man who had found himself denied a possession he desired and had decided to do something about it. Rafael Vives, even in his role of so-called gardener, was a man who would always do something about getting what he wanted.

'And what are you expecting now?' Amy asked quietly. 'Now that you've put yourself through all *this*?'

'I don't know what I expect…' He had known up until she had laid into him like a ton of bricks. Now he just knew what he wanted. 'But what I want is for you to give this a chance…'

'By which I guess you mean we should head up to the nearest bedroom, rip each other's clothes off and make love. If you were so desperate for my wonderful company, why did it take you so long to work your way over to England?'

'I needed to try…to get you out of my system…' For Rafael, that was an almighty admission. Since he had never had any woman *in* his system, he had never had to try to get any woman *out* of it. Just confessing to the weakness made him feel exposed.

What Amy heard was the statement of a man who had tried all right…tried to do what he sensibly wanted to do, which would have been to forget her because she was, face it, inappropriate. As inappropriate for him as she had been for his brother. His *half*-brother, as he kept pointing out, as though it made the slightest bit of difference. She had listened to his brief life history just then, which he had offered to explain, she supposed, the marked difference in their appearances, the difference in their surnames, Rafael having kept the one he was born with. The only thing she had been capable of thinking was that he had lied to her.

'But I couldn't.'

'Too bad,' Amy said sarcastically. 'Bit of a nuisance having to traipse over here to work this out of your system.' He made her sound like an infectious disease that had to be cleared up as quickly as possible. 'Did you set aside some time for the purpose? Say a couple of weeks? That should just about get your life back to normal and you can disappear back to New York to pick up where you left off before I came along. And where, incidentally, *would* that place be?'

'Look, Amy…'

'No, *don't*!' She stood up. There were bright patches of colour in her cheeks. The anger was building up inside her again, like a volcano working itself up to another eruption. 'I told you *everything* about myself! And you sat there, listening, pretending to be interested, when in fact you were only interested in picking up clues so that you could protect your bank balance! Is that why you slept with me, Rafael? To try and drive James out of my head?'

'Don't be ridiculous.' Rafael flushed darkly. Every accusation had just a shameful tinge of truth behind it. Somewhere in the recesses of his mind, he remembered having thought just that, but that had been before he had lost control of the situation had and the situation started to control *him*.

'Don't you *dare* tell me that I'm being ridiculous!'

'You are the most frustrating woman on the face of the earth!'

'Would that be because I'm not afraid to have a point of view? Especially when I'm at the receiving end of a raw deal? I can just imagine why you would have told me that I wasn't your type! I bet the women you like never raise their voices because who would dare raise their voice to a tycoon like you? You must have had a good laugh at my expense with your brother,' Amy finished wearily. 'Did you call him every night with updates on how it was going?'

'That is an insult.'

'No, it's not.' Yes, it was. 'You lied to me. I don't even know who you are now. Who are you? The man who owns all this…' She spread her arms to encompass the luxurious house, just one, she supposed, of many scattered across the globe. 'Or the man with nothing?'

'Same man,' Rafael told her grimly. This, he thought, was not going to work. He shouldn't have pursued this woman in the first place. She was right. He wasn't going to commit to her so what had been the point of the chase? 'I lied to you. Whether you accept the apology or not is incidental because you were damned right on one score. Neither of us needs this. I shouldn't have come over here. It was a mistake. I won't drop you home. There's no point prolonging the inevitable. I'll get my driver to take you back and, before you launch into another outraged monologue on yet more things I possess, yes, I have a driver. Or, should I say, I use the guy who works for the company directors but my priorities take precedence over theirs. Also this magnificent house is mine even though I rarely use it. I also have houses in Paris and the Caribbean. If I'm an unforgivable liar to be defined by the possessions I didn't tell you about, then you might as well know them all. You can go away then and stew over the narrow escape you had from getting involved with a man like me.'

Yes! That should have made her feel a lot better! It didn't. There was no more arguing to be done and she realised that he now wanted to get rid of her. She had shrieked once too often. Not that she didn't have a point, she thought bitterly. But then why did she feel so empty as she was bundled into the back of the Jag? She wanted to turn back for one last glimpse, but when she did he had disappeared back into the house.

CHAPTER NINE

AMY expected Rafael to be on the first plane back to America. She wouldn't have dreamed of actually making an effort to find out, of phoning James and casually dropping the question into the conversation, even though she was racked with misery and barely functioning. The only reason she found out was because, three weeks after she had been ejected from his house, she happened to open the newspaper and there, wedged at the back in those boring financial pages she usually avoided like the plague, was a picture of him smiling, with a tall, dark-haired woman lightly leaning into him, also smiling.

She read the article over and over, stared at the picture repeatedly, even holding it up to the light and squinting to see if she could decipher any expression on his face that might give her an inkling of what was going through his head. She scrutinised his well-groomed partner and tried to pretend that she was fine with the idea of him with another woman. He was footloose and fancy-free, after all, and how could she complain when she had been the one to send him on his merry way?

It seemed that Rafael Vives, as the chairman and major shareholder of his vast, listed company, had decided to relocate to London for a six-month tenure, during which he intended to sell off certain bits of the company so that he could extend his fledgling venture into the leisure industry. There were all sorts of sums and figures and detailed analysis, which Amy assumed other financial people were interested in, but the only other fact she wanted to know was the identity of the brunette.

She binned the newspaper article, only to retrieve it from underneath the potato peelings three hours later. Then she proceeded to stew over it for three days.

Her lethargy gave way to furious activity. That feeling of being half dead disappeared. In its place was a frantic, restless energy that left her exhausted at the end of the day.

She had stuck the article on her fridge with a magnet. In the mornings, before she left for her course, she had a bowl of cereal and glowered at it from the kitchen table. In the evenings, over elaborate meals that she cooked for practice only to nibble her way through half, she did the same.

Two weeks of this saw her teetering on the edge of complete meltdown before she did the unthinkable. She picked up the phone and called James.

She said all the usual things to him, told him that she was making sure he didn't forget her name because, when she began her apprenticeship at one of the leading London hotels, she just wanted to know that he would come along and sample her offerings. She whittered on about wanting to open her own restaurant and was chuffed when he told her that he would happily sink some money in the venture, to just let him know where and when. Which actually made her stop and think that perhaps she would indeed do that, open a restaurant, instead of just hanging on to a pipedream that would never materialise in a month of Sundays.

Then, almost as an afterthought, she mentioned that she had read in the newspapers that his brother had decided to relocate to London for a few weeks to work.

'About time he used that house of his,' James joked. ''ve been there a couple of times and it's like a mausoleum—not that it'll stay like that for very long. Elizabeth will soon put that right.'

'Elizabeth?' Amy felt the blood rush to her head and thanked the Lord that she wasn't having this conversation with him face to face.

'Oh, sorry. Have I been tactless? I knew you and he were involved…had something going on…'

'Oh, good heavens! Brief fling, James. Very brief! In fact, I haven't given your brother a passing thought until I saw that article in the newspapers about him the other day.'

'Which article? There've been a few. When Rafael puts his mind to it, the whole world stops and listens and right now they're listening hard because his next step might have a big impact on the stock markets.'

'Oh, right, sure.' Amy wondered how to steer the conversation away from the deadly subject of stock markets and back to the more pressing topic of Elizabeth. Who the heck was *Elizabeth*? How on earth could Rafael have met a woman in such a short space of time?

Then she remembered his vast millions. The sort of vast millions that could pull any woman from any distance in any country. Add his killer looks to the equation and what did you have? An Elizabeth.

'He used to go out with Elizabeth in New York,' James was saying. Amy tuned into the conversation and held her breath.

'Really?' She tried to maintain just the right level of polite interest that would get him to expand on the subject, but he didn't. He wound up their conversation, just, she thought regretfully, when it was getting interesting, by telling her to keep in touch and to call him as soon as she decided on that restaurant of hers. If they decided to really expand in the leisure industry, there would be an opening for a fresh new chef to head up their restaurants.

'Brilliant!' Of course she knew where the mysterious Elizabeth would be staying. Where else but Rafael's luxurious house in the heart of the city? And she wasn't going to give him up, not without a fight.

Yes, the sensible side of her was telling her that it would be a pointless fight. Yes, every single member of her family, with whom she had shared her problem, had advised her to focus on her career and save the heartbreak for later.

Unfortunately, another less well-behaved side of her was telling her that her life had been miserable for the past few weeks and what the heck? Either she tried to be the stoic person she had never in her life been or else she just gave in and tried her damnedest to win him back. Her pride would take a beating, but suffering for the sake of pride seemed a painful, uphill struggle.

She came off the phone with just the vaguest skeleton of a plan forming in her head.

It might take a bit of sneaking around and calling in favours owed and, when she thought about it, she felt sick inside, but then when she thought about the endless empty days stretching in front of her, she felt even sicker.

Claire still worked at the company. So far, Amy had tried to keep a lid on her curiosity. She had avoided asking her friend any questions about Rafael. Her reasons for this were twofold. Firstly, she had been desperate not to appear desperate, and secondly, she knew that just one whiff of interest and Claire would unleash a torrent of questions. She knew the basic facts of the fated affair but Amy's silence on the subject had made it difficult to get down to the nitty gritty.

She resolved to at least think things over for a day or two but in the end that noble resolution lasted just as long as it took her to have a bath. Then, with her towel still wrapped around her, she was on the phone to Claire, bypassing the usual pleasant gossip and getting straight to the point.

'So let me get this straight,' Claire rounded up, when she was finally satisfied with Amy's thrilling agenda, 'you want me to find out his movements and let you know.'

'Shouldn't be too hard,' Amy said airily. She started thinking about Rafael's possible reaction to her cunning plan, but didn't spend too much time dwelling on that particular thought. It was a little too scary. 'You can potter around that directors' floor with a tray of sandwiches in your hand and ferret out the information from Jules.'

'Jules doesn't work for him. Some new woman does and she looks the sort that eats small children for breakfast.'

'Well, I'll leave it to you. Honestly, Claire, it's not as though you haven't done the odd underhand thing in your time!'

'I'll try my best. But there's a price to pay. You'll have to tell me *everything* that goes on, leaving *nothing* out, and also invite me to the wedding.'

'Yes to the first two and, ha, ha, what a good joke to the last.' Amy wasn't born yesterday. She wasn't looking for love and marriage. She was just looking for a way to get the man out of her system. She had fallen hopelessly in love with him and had turned him away because she had wanted so much more than he was offering. She had now had ample opportunity to experience that vicious little emotion called *regret*. It was the thing that woke her up early on a Sunday morning and filled her head so that relaxing and having fun was a distant memory.

'You can never tell,' Claire said, but she sounded doubtful. But she did it. She came up trumps after two nail-biting days for Amy as she tossed up in her mind the pros and cons of what she intended to do.

Wednesday. He would be working late. She knew that because he was chairing a meeting for all the directors, which wasn't due to finish until eight-thirty, but instead of leaving with them he would be continuing work at his desk. He had asked her, via his battleaxe of a personal assistant, to make sure that something was prepared for him to snack on if he felt so inclined.

Like a Lord giving his orders, Amy thought. Get me a snack and so it shall be done!

When she joked about it in her head, she could almost believe that she couldn't possibly have fallen for him. How could she have when she was so *different*? But she always ended up with the same realisation—that love didn't always obey the rules your head laid down. Sometimes it broke its leash and galloped all over the place until there was nothing to do but go along for the ride, just as she was doing, never mind the broken bones later.

Which was why she was swallowing back good old common sense and doing something that went totally against the grain.

She only hoped, as Wednesday dawned, that there would be no change of plan.

She didn't need the trauma of bumping into anyone, all of whom would recognise her, and Claire, having delivered on her promise, had refused to go that one step further and act as lookout.

So nine o'clock saw Amy chatting to the guy on Reception, who recognised her and helpfully asked no awkward questions.

Then she skulked her way up to the directors' floor, avoiding the lift because she had visions of the lift door opening to reveal James and his band of merry men on their way to their Covent Garden restaurant.

It was quiet. The meeting was definitely done and dusted because she passed by the boardroom, which bore the cluttered detritus of debate. The pads of paper, pens and pencils randomly scattered, the projector still in its position though switched off. By nine the next morning, the room would be pristine, cleaned to within an inch of its life.

Amy padded past the boardroom, skirted around the small, central foyer, which was arranged as an informal sitting area where casual meetings were sometimes held, and followed her nose and then, eventually, saw the glimmer of light coming from an office at the end. She knew the floor very well indeed and so also knew, immediately, that the office Rafael was occupying belonged to James. Poor old James had been relegated, although. remembering his admiring tone of voice as he had chatted to her about Rafael and his big plans, she didn't suppose he minded too much.

She paused when she was standing by the door, out of sight with the chance to change her mind still within reach.

Before she could take the coward's way out, she stepped into the doorway and had a few seconds in which to observe him because he hadn't seen her. His head was bent and he was frowning and tapping on a little pile of papers with the top of his pen.

Rafael Vives, gardener. Rafael Vives, multimillionaire. He had told her that he was the same man but it was hard not to be disconcerted by the aura of power he exuded, which was crazy, especially when you considered that she had slept with this man, laughed with him, forced him to buy a pair of jeans!

She gave a little cough and he looked up.

He was as damn near shocked to see her as it was probably possible for him to be, and in that fraction of time she jumped in before he had time to speak.

Amy hadn't actually planned what she was going to say. At least not in any detail. She had just pretty much decided that she would proceed on a wing and a prayer.

'I heard you'd decided to stay on in London for a while,' she said, stepping into the lion's den and shutting the door behind her only to immediately wonder whether that had been a bad move. 'And I was in the area so I thought I'd drop by…' She looked at his heart-stoppingly sexy face and wondered how she was going to deal with it if he chucked her out. No questions asked.

'Oh, really.' Rafael pushed himself away from the desk so that he could recline back and give her his full and undivided attention. 'You were just *passing by,* were you? On the way to where exactly?'

'Oh…home…you know…'

'No, actually, I don't but we'll let that one ride. You've dropped in…for what reason?'

'Would you mind if I sat down?'

'You won't be staying so what's the point?'

Amy sagged. 'You're right. What's the point?'

'What did you come for?' Rafael had cancelled Elizabeth because he had too much work to do. Right now she would be waiting for him at the house, having had a heavy day sight-seeing. Two weeks' vacation, a chance to mend the broken fences between them, and what was he doing? Spending most of his available free time at work. He disliked himself for it but the reconciliation was turning out to be a disaster. Their relationship was flat and he should have left it alone.

'I came to find out how you were and I wish I hadn't bothered, to be perfectly honest.'

'What did you expect?' Rafael's voice was cold and dismissive but he could feel the anger building up inside him and he was annoyed with himself because he didn't want to feel angry. He wanted her to stay in the box he had made, somewhere at the back of his mind. A nice, safe distance away, somewhere he could label 'history'. He could control the situation then. 'Did you expect the red carpet to be rolled out in your welcome?'

'No, but a little politeness might have been nice!' Shrieking again, Amy thought. What was it with this man? 'I'm sorry. I shouldn't have come.'

'How did you know that I had decided to stay on?'

'Claire. Claire told me. Remember her? She came out to the Hamptons on that company trip…' She had a vivid burst of memories and had to drag herself back to the present and back to the intransigent man sitting in front of her. It was one thing to think about fighting for the person you loved, but it was quite a different matter when the person in question didn't want the fight. In fact, just wanted to be left alone.

'Company spy.'

'Hardly.'

'You mean you asked her about me?'

'No! She just sort of mentioned it in passing…' She hoped she wasn't in the process of landing her friend in a mess, but confessing to reading about him in the newspaper would entail her having to explain that she knew that he was involved with someone, and there was no way she intended letting him know that she had quizzed his brother either. No way.

'I was curious, that's all. To find out why you had decided to stay on.'

'Because you thought that I had made a trip to London specifically to pursue you?'

'I never thought that! Anyway…I'll be off.' She turned around, defeated, and headed back towards the door. If she had sat down like a normal person and thought her crazy idea through instead of just rushing in on impulse, she realised she might have predicted its outcome. She had turned him away and he wasn't just going to forgive and forget. His ego had probably been wounded and, even if the damage had been temporary, he would still have been hard-pressed to forgive her because men notoriously had very fragile egos. And a rich man's ego would be particularly fragile, she guessed, because he would be so unaccustomed to having it wounded.

'I'd been thinking of branching out for a while.' Rafael arrested her in her flight towards the door. 'London seemed a more controllable market than the US, with more scope of innovation, hence the trip over here.' He wanted to make that perfectly clear, even though it was a complete fabrication. He had actually planned to return to America immediately, but in the wake of her outraged reaction to his duplicity he had found himself temporarily rudderless, and into the unaccustomed vacuum the idea had taken root and solidified as something very much worth doing. It also, strangely, allowed him to prove to himself that his movements weren't going to be dictated by some woman he had happened to meet by chance and with whom he had had an ill-advised fling.

That would have been pretty hard for him to swallow!

'Oh. Good,' Amy said vaguely, as always losing interest the minute any talk of finance reared its head.

'Yes. Elizabeth thinks so as well…'

'Elizabeth?' She marshalled her thoughts and tried to sound as though the name meant nothing to her at all. 'Who's Elizabeth?'

'The woman I'm going out with.' Rafael couldn't help the little kick of satisfaction at Amy's reaction. Of course he was an adult and a serious one at that, not one to play games, never had been, but he had to admit that embellishing his story was tempting. 'I knew her over in New York. Went out with her for a while, as a matter of fact, then we decided that we both needed space from one another.'

'Which was when you met me?'

'Yes.'

'And now you've had your fling with me, you've decided that it's time to get back together with you ex.' The fighter in her kicked in. She remembered that she was here to try and win him back because without him her life was empty. She nodded sagely and edged towards the chair. Okay, he had told her not to make herself comfortable because she wouldn't be staying long, but she wasn't going to have an emotional conversation standing up.

'What does that nod mean?' Rafael asked suspiciously.

'Can I interest you in a drink somewhere? Or something to eat? If you haven't eaten already?'

Rafael had planned on working steadily for the next hour or so, even though he was guiltily aware that Elizabeth would be on her own for the evening. However, he hadn't banked on this little slice of his past dropping in to pay him a visit. And he didn't know *why*. He didn't believe any rubbish about *being in the area*. Oh, no. She was here for a reason and his curiosity was just too strong to resist. He stood up and nodded briefly.

'I was on my way out, as a matter of fact, so why not? A quick drink for old times' sake.'

'So, nice for you to have your girlfriend here with you,' Amy said, just as soon as they were in the lift. 'Although I *do* find it a bit odd that you would seek me out and ask me over when, presumably, you were thinking about getting back together with your ex. Why would you do that?'

Amy had always left the running to the boys. It was ingrained in her that they should be the ones who did the chasing. But really, she thought, why should they? In every other area of her life she had been taught to believe that if she wanted something, then she should pursue her goal because she was capable of getting anything she wanted. Her parents had given her the gift of self-confidence. Why shouldn't she use that now to pursue the one thing in life she really wanted, which was *him*? So it wasn't going to be easy, but she could try, couldn't she? She could try and win the man she loved and wanted?

'Maybe you did me the favour of making me realise that good sex is one thing but long-lasting companionship is something else and long lasting companionship, for me at least, has to be with a woman who doesn't spend most of her time shouting.'

Amy took a deep breath and resolved not to shout even though she wanted to. She hung onto the 'good sex' bit of his sentence. It wasn't what she wanted but, having rejected it, she had now discovered that it was, actually, better than nothing.

'You know, they say that shouting is actually very good for the soul.'

'Really. I haven't heard that one.' They were walking now towards the wine bar frequented by the people who worked in the city. Rafael glanced at his watch and knew that he shouldn't be doing this. He should be heading back to the house where he would doubtless find Elizabeth patiently waiting for him. They would discuss, sensibly, how each other's days had gone and she would ask him informed questions about the progression of his current deals. He, in turn, would ask her about the two cases she had left behind and which he knew were bothering her.

She wouldn't be *winding him up*.

'Yep. It's true. Absolutely. If you don't shout you lose touch with your *id,* which is, apparently, the bit of us that's *alive* and *vital.*'

'I've never heard such a lot of nonsense in my life,' Rafael told her, but he felt like grinning. 'Do you want a glass of wine?'

'Okay.' She watched as he strolled off to the bar. She wondered how she could have reacted so strongly to the fact that he had hidden the truth from her, had led her to believe that he was someone he wasn't. He had only been trying to protect his brother from someone who could have turned out to be a scheming gold-digger. She would probably have done the same in his shoes! She tried to imagine what it might feel like to be fabulously rich and driven to be suspicious of anyone who hadn't been carefully vetted, but she just couldn't get her head around the concept.

Anyway, there was the more pressing matter of how she was going to retrace her steps and try and persuade him into an affair after all. When he was obviously reluctant. And when there was a girlfriend on the scene.

However tenacious Amy was, she couldn't bring herself to think that all was fair in love and war. She thought how *she* would feel were she stuck in a foreign country, hoping to make a relationship work, while out there some ex-fling was sharpening her hooks and sizing up her man as a potential target.

But what could be the harm in finding out a little more about this mystery woman? Whether Rafael wanted to admit it or not, he couldn't be *that* keen on her, could he? Not if he had already dumped her once! Ha!

Amy clung to this thought like a drowning man clinging to a lifebelt.

'So,' she said as soon as he had handed her her glass, 'what's she like?'

'Elizabeth? Why are you interested? Is that why you descended on me out of the blue? To find out why I was still around and whether I was seeing anyone?' He looked at her carefully.

'Okay. I'll confess. I saw your picture in the newspaper a few days ago. There was a long article about you staying on to do something or other…'

'Still right up there with the financial news, I see.'

'And you had a tall brunette swaying on your arm.'

Elizabeth, Rafael thought, didn't *sway.*

'And so you just gave in to curiosity and poled up at my

office to find out what was going on. Even though it's none of your business.'

Amy tried and failed to find a reasonable answer to that.

'Well, Elizabeth is…a glamorous, independent woman with a thriving career in law. An attorney, in fact, on course to become a judge before she's forty.'

'Oh.' Suddenly the mountain she had set forth to climb seemed impossibly steep. 'Not the sort, I guess, who watches reality TV and takes two weeks to work out her bank balance.'

'Not that sort, no.'

'How did you meet? Were you…going out with her when…when we…'

'No.' Rafael's voice was sharp.

'You must have had a surprise when you met me,' Amy said with a wistful smile. 'I guess Elizabeth doesn't do much tree-climbing.'

'Or getting lost because she's trying to walk off an agitated frame of mind.'

'No.' She wondered how she could ever have thought that she could *fight for this man*! 'Why did you break up with her?'

Rafael shrugged. He had a pretty valid argument for saying nothing because his relationship was none of her business, but, hell, it must have taken guts to come to his office when she would have known that his reaction would fall far short of welcoming. And to make it obvious that she wanted him back.

'We needed a break from each other. We both lead high-octane lives and we'd got into the habit of seeing each other on the run. No way for a relationship to work.'

Amy wondered whether the time they had spent together, when he had abandoned his *high-octane* life and taken time out, had been instrumental in propelling him back to his ex. She thought that if she was a generous person she would have been pleased to have inadvertently brought two people back together. Instead she decided that she was pretty mean spirited after all because she just wished the wretched woman had remained where she was, safely out of the picture.

So what if she wasn't Rafael's lifetime soul mate? So what if the attorney who never got lost was more his cup of tea? She, Amy, would have just enjoyed what she had got and moved on when he decided that he wanted to go back where he belonged. When he had talked about 'unfinished business', instead of jumping up and down and clamouring on about being deceived, she should have realised that he had a point. But as always she had reacted without bothering to think things through.

'I'm surprised she managed to take time out of the high-octane life,' Amy said sourly. 'Is she getting withdrawal symptoms?'

'I'm making sure to ease them,' Rafael said, feeling the thrill of the victor when her expression tightened.

'Would that be by leaving her on her own while you have a drink with me?'

Rafael looked at the wild blonde hair, the cute, expressive face and marvelled at how she could make him feel so primitive. 'Which reminds me. I have to go.' He drained his glass and stood up. The gentleman in him fought to remember that he had a girlfriend waiting for him, an intelligent, decent woman who deserved to be treated with respect.

'But first…' He stuck his hands in his pockets and waited while she wriggled into her little cropped jacket. It was cold outside but she was still wearing a pair of jeans that sat a few indecent inches below her belly button and a long-sleeved top that refused to stay put and insisted on revealing her flat, smooth stomach. Rafael dragged his eyes away. 'Tell me why you needed to find out about Elizabeth.'

'Because I've spent too long…' she pushed open the door

and was rewarded with darkness outside so that he was unable to see the expression on her face '…*way* too long thinking about you. Okay, I admit you…hurt me.' She looked up at him and was annoyed that the darkness also hid *his* expression. What if he was stifling a yawn? 'Nobody likes to feel that they've been lied to and nobody likes to feel that someone else thinks that they're a gold-digger.'

'So what are you doing here?' Rafael asked.

'Oh, I came to try and win you back,' Amy said casually. She stuck out her hand to hail a cab. 'I realised that I could stick to my guns and be too proud to ever make contact with you again or else I could swallow my pride and give us a stab…but that was before…'

Rafael curled his fingers round her wrist and pulled her hand down to his side. 'Before what?'

'Before I…talked to you,' Amy said on a sigh. She did look at him now. 'I didn't realise how keen you were on your ex-girlfriend. Actually, when you described her, I could see that she was a woman perfectly suited to you. She even kind of *looks* like you! Tall and composed and dark-haired. But more important than that, she *thinks* like you. I bet she actually *understands* when you start talking about the *World Economy*!' This had been a small joke between them, the fact that she knew so little about how world finances worked. At the time she had been amused that he would take such an interest in something so far removed from gardening as economics and had cheerfully believed him when he had told her that that was precisely *why* he found it so interesting. 'I bet she doesn't yawn and her eyes don't glaze over when you start trying to make her understand that money markets actually make sense!'

Rafael grunted his agreement with this observation. If his ego had been dented by her refusal all those weeks ago, he should have been feeling pleasantly vindicated by her standing in front of him, eyes wide, happily prostrating herself for his benefit. Well, he was, he decided. He still had his fingers curled around her wrist. She had thin wrists. In fact, he could probably circle her upper arm if he wanted to.

'If you'd been seeing someone…you obviously didn't admire so much…who wasn't so *suited* to you…' She sighed heavily and chewed her lip.

'You would have tried to steal me away?'

'Not to the land of commitment,' Amy said quickly. 'I know we're not really on the same wavelength, but you were right…maybe it would have been better not to have this feeling of unfinished business between us. Not,' she amended hastily, just in case he thought that she was still going to pursue him, like some kind of lunatic stalker, 'that that applies to you. You've found the woman of your dreams and, honestly, Rafael, I wish you all the best.'

She stood on tiptoe and placed the palms of her hands squarely on his chest. Just one peck on his cheek. A friendly, supportive kiss. Just something to show him that she was a good loser, even if it hurt like hell.

Rafael tensed at the casual touch. Up close, the smell of her was insinuating, that light, clean, flowery smell, which surely must have been aided and abetted by some sort of perfume. He was unaware of himself automatically reaching to cup her elbows and steady her, unaware of looking down to her soft face and hardly conscious at all of capturing her mouth with his, turning the friendly peck on the cheek into a light kiss that deepened, and deepened until it drove every sane thought out of his head.

He came to his senses abruptly. Amy, still absorbed in the wonder of kissing him, felt him stiffen and pull away and, of course, so did she.

'Don't say *anything*, Rafael.' She drew back and stuck her hand out to hail a cab. It was still very busy on the roads. Surely an empty one would cruise up to her and spare her the indignity of drawing out this uncomfortable little scene.

Luck was with her. 'We kissed and I'm glad we did, but that doesn't mean that I don't wish you happiness because I do. Everyone deserves a suitable partner and you've found yours.' She rattled off the sentence and neatly finished just in time to fling open the door of the cab and slip inside. He had no time to say anything and Amy was very pleased about that because she didn't want to hear him berate himself for having done something he shouldn't have done, or, worse, try and lay the blame at *her* door.

Once again she was leaving and once again she wasn't going to look back.

CHAPTER TEN

FROM the bottom of his glass, Rafael slowly and inexorably worked out what had been happening to him. He had opened the bottle of whisky intending to drown his restless, frustrated energy the good, old fashioned way, but in all events had ended up having just the one glass.

The house still had the detritus of Elizabeth's rapid departure the day before. From where he sat in the kitchen, there were still pots and pans in the sink, waiting to be washed. If he looked in the fridge, he knew he would find an assortment of healthy-eating options and cartons of freshly squeezed orange juice. There was a time when he had appreciated her discipline when it came to her diet. He didn't know what had possessed him to think that, having become bored with it all, he might retrieve his original feelings once again. Had he thought that England would revitalise their relationship?

He twirled the glass in his hand and stared down at the dregs of the whisky and soda.

The fact was that had he never had his life changed, disrupted, *steamrollered,* call it what you would, by a slight-figured, fair-haired witch, he might well have returned to Elizabeth and married her because she was so eminently *right* for him, at least on paper.

Rafael had always been amused but disapproving of his younger brother's playboy ways. Just as he had always been privately disdainful of the women James attached himself to. He had met a fair few of them and had considered them all, without exception, shallow, never mind how they looked. He, Rafael Vives, had not only kept his Spanish surname but, it had to be said, thought himself a man of more gravitas than his brother. James advertised, but he, Rafael, was the mover and shaker behind the scenes.

And then Amy had stormed into his well ordered life and turned it upside down.

She was so far removed from his ideal of the perfect woman for him that he had utterly failed to notice the way she had insinuated herself under his skin so that in the space of a few short days she had taken over his head.

He resisted the urge to pour himself another drink and instead helped himself to some bottled water. They lined one entire shelf of his fridge like little soldiers and, as he'd expected, the rest of the shelves were stuffed with lettuce, vegetables, fruit, yoghurts. A jar of olives peeked out from behind some salad dressing. It seemed to sum up his relationship with Elizabeth. How could she not have known that he *hated* olives?

He drank the water in one go and then went to get his car. He knew that he could spare himself the tedium of dealing with the London traffic by calling his driver, but the last thing he needed was a witness to his potential embarrassment because, face it, he thought to himself, why should Amy take him back when he had politely, yet again, sent her on her way? After she had debased herself by coming to him, offering herself on his terms? She might not have *loved* him, but she had been willing to explore what they had and he had turned her away because, fool that he was, he hadn't been able to conceive of himself as a man who could possibly want to explore any kind of relationship with a woman who wasn't as substantial as the ones he had made a habit of dating.

Never mind that she was warm and funny and quirky and could make him forget that the only thing he loved was his work. Never mind that she could make him play truant, entice him into making love in extraordinary places, turn him on even when she was irritating the hell out of him.

He thought of Elizabeth and deeply regretted the hurt he knew he would have caused her, but she had taken it well, just as he had expected her to. No shouting or screaming.

'I don't think this is going to work, after all,' he said, and she looked at him calmly, her head tilted to one side, and nodded.

'But we gave it one last shot, Rafael,' she said sadly, smiling, which made him feel even more of a cad. 'I think, all things considered, that it's probably best if I leave…' and he nodded, all very controlled. He even offered to help her pack her things was relieved when she quietly turned down the offer.

It had been so *civilised*. Right now, she was staying at a hotel until she could get her flight changed. He wouldn't have been surprised if she decided to stay on a few more days because why ever not? There were still things to see in London before she left and, above all else, Elizabeth was sensible.

He took the drive to Amy's house very slowly. He had had a full day to try and figure himself out. Now, it was dark and cold, which was a much better time to do what he had to do.

As usual, there was no hurrying the traffic. Like New York, London never seemed to do a great deal of sleeping, least of all at seven-thirty in the evening.

He finally pulled up outside her house and killed the engine. Closing a deal had always sent a rush of adrenaline through him. Moving and investing vast sums of money had likewise given him the same surge of excitement. Neither had ever made him feel as sickeningly vulnerable as he did now, staring up at her front door in the darkness.

He wondered whether the outcome of his visit to London would have been different had he approached her in a different way. Instead of enticing her to his house under false pretences, mistakenly thinking that she would see the element of surprise as flattering, maybe he should just have telephoned her, suggested meeting up on neutral ground, and then confessed to her that he had been a fool, that he wanted her so much that it was driving him crazy, that they could solve the problem of distance one way or another. Perhaps honesty would have been the best policy. Which led him to think about what he was going to say to her now.

He would tell her straight away that Elizabeth was no longer on the scene. That bit, he thought, would be the easiest. Less easy would be when he started talking to her about his feelings.

Rafael frowned. Where, he wondered, did a man start when it came to discussing *feelings*?

He imagined James would be pretty good in that area. He, on the other hand, tended to be more prosaic. He also wasn't entirely sure how much of those feelings he was inclined to reveal. Honesty was one thing, but he also needed to protect himself.

He was sitting in the car, flirting with his delaying tactics, when a movement interrupted his line of vision. Not that he had been looking at anything in particular. Just absent-mindedly looking in the general direction of her house.

It took a couple of seconds for him to register that her front door was opening, that she was standing at it, that she was with a man. And the man was sticking on his coat, patting his pockets as though feeling for something.

Rafael found himself fascinated by the unfolding tableau. In his head, he had been prepared for pretty much anything, including having the crockery thrown at his repentant head.

What he hadn't banked on was to find a man emerging from her house. There had been no recent ex in the background. So who the hell was he?

Jealousy, an emotion he had never had much time for, slammed into him with such force that he actually gasped. Then he was opening his door, at much the same time as the man was leaning into her, enfolding her in an embrace that spoke of pure intimacy.

He didn't think he was running, but he must have been because they both detached themselves to look in the direction of his feet pounding along the pavement.

Rafael had only ever been involved in a fight once before in his life. He had been a teenager at the time and a remark had been made about his nationality. The passing remark had led onto further insulting remarks and the raucous jeering had triggered something in him that had made him see red. He had piled into the lot of them single-handedly and had only emerged from the fracas when they had scattered to the four winds. A bloody victor. It had been an ugly scene and the loss of self-control had been a brutal learning curve for him. Yes, his mother and stepfather had given him the expected lecture about rising to taunts, about physical violence not being the answer to anything. In actual fact, they need not have bothered because it was a lesson he had learnt for himself.

He could feel the lesson flying out the window as he reached forward and grabbed the man by the lapels of his coat to slam him back against the wall while Amy tried to yank him off.

He was aware that people were staring and he propelled the man back into the house, with Amy still ineffectively trying to prise him off, then he kicked the door shut behind him with one foot.

'Right,' he said grimly, 'who the hell are you and what are you doing here?'

'Will you *let him go*?' Amy screeched from behind him. Rafael ignored her. Every ounce of his concentration was fixed on the terrified, confused face of the man who seemed to have lost the power of speech.

'Listen, mate.'

'I'm not your *mate*,' Rafael bit out, keeping his voice under control and his fist too, even though he wanted to lay into the guy, who, it had to be said, was no match for him physically. A good few inches shorter and slight in comparison to Rafael's muscular build.

'Look, just let me go and…'

Then there was a jumble of words, with the man begging to be released and scrabbling to find some kind of vantage point, Amy yelling at Rafael, asking him what in heck was he doing and Rafael informing the man, still in a very controlled voice, that he was going to dump him outside and letting Amy know that he had every intention of finding out what some guy was doing under her roof.

Amy assured her brother she was fine and then turned to Rafael, hands on her hips, every inch of her bristling in stupefied anger.

She made for the door and Rafael's arm shot out, barring her way.

'No chance. You're not going anywhere until you tell me who that was.'

He removed his coat and pitched it over the banister. Yes, he was calming down, but, no, he wasn't going to feel guilty about what he had done even though she was looking at him with those huge, enraged eyes.

'Who do you think you *are,* Rafael Vives? Barging into my house like that! How *dare* you?'

'How the hell am I supposed to react when I find you making out with some man in your doorway!' Especially when you're dressed like that, he thought savagely, in a tight little pair of faded jeans and a tight, old long-sleeved tee shirt under which it's obvious you're not wearing a bloody bra…

He raked his fingers through his hair and glared at her. 'He should be lucky I didn't thump him.'

'You still haven't told me what you're doing here!'

'And you still haven't told me who that was!' Rafael responded without pausing for breath.

They were standing in the hall like combatants. Amy, still in a state of shock, had a thousand questions burning in her head but she was done with laying all her cards on the table and putting herself at his mercy. Never again!

She swung round and padded towards the kitchen, really because she needed to sit down because her legs felt like jelly.

She was aware of Rafael following her. It made the hairs on the back of her neck stand on end.

'Well?' he demanded, as soon as they were in the kitchen. She sat down but he remained standing, giving him a towering advantage over her.

'It's none of your business who that was,' Amy said bitterly. 'There's nothing more to be said between us.'

'And so you decided to just head out and find another man?'

Yes! Amy wanted to shout. Yes, I did. Just walked out one fine morning and picked up the first guy who strolled along and offered to go on a date!

'Is that the kind of woman you think I am? No, don't answer that! Because once you thought I was a gold-digger, so I guess I'm just about capable of anything, in your eyes!' Which is why you wouldn't dream of looking at me as anything other than a quick and easy romp in the sack! 'Where's the love of your life?' she asked snidely. 'Don't tell me you've abandoned her again! I hate to say this but even the most controlled, well-bred, intelligent women with power jobs have a breaking-point.'

Rafael shook his head and sat down. 'Elizabeth has gone.'

Huh, Amy thought, would that be so that she can begin preparing for The Big Day?

'I finished with her.'

'What?' She looked at him warily. She could feel her treacherous heart lifting and tried hard to stamp it back down.

'It didn't work out. I thought it would but I was wrong.'

She was desperate to know the details, but she hung onto her resolve and just stared at him in silence.

'Now tell me who he was, Amy.' Even applying his cool, logical brain to the question of what he would do if she started spilling out details of her new lover, he still couldn't control the sick surge that rushed through him, leaving him shaken in its wake.

'Oh, for goodness' sake, Rafael!' The sweet fantasy of being able to exclaim that she had just so happened to meet the man of her dreams regrettably evaporated. 'That was just Jack, my brother.'

'Your *brother*!

'Who's probably bruised and shaken, thanks to you!'

'Why the hell didn't you tell me who he was?'

'Because you didn't exactly give me much of a chance, did you?' She fuelled her anger and tried to feel some justified horror at the way he was coolly sitting at her table. 'I mean, one minute my brother was giving me a hug and the next minute you were attacking him! Tell me where you see polite conversation and explanations fitting into that little scenario!'

'Point taken,' Rafael said. Her brother. He was her brother. The man was her brother. He couldn't believe the relief he felt! He wanted to jump up and down and dance. Ridiculous reaction. Just as laying into her brother had been a ridiculous reaction. Not *him* at all! But then, nothing was these days, was it?

'I shouldn't have attacked him, even if I *had* thought that you had found someone else, found a replacement for me…'

If only life were that simple, Amy thought glumly.

'Why did you?' she asked eventually. 'I mean, don't you hate causing scenes? All that passion and emotion on show, Rafael! I would never have thought it of you! But then, no, let me answer my own question…' She looked at him bitterly. 'You thought that was what I might want to see. You thought that because I'm open and expressive, that I would be bowled over by a Rafael who didn't mind showing his feelings. A brand-new Rafael. Because you've given your ex a chance and you've decided that you'd rather use me for a while, even though I'm not up to scratch on the permanent front. Am I heading in the right direction, Rafael?'

Amy stood up abruptly. Her legs felt like pieces of lead and she needed to walk to get her circulation going.

Also she didn't want to look at him. Unfortunately the kitchen was small. Not too many spots from which she didn't have a full on, glaring view of him, lounging against the counter and dwarfing everything around him.

Which really just left the option of heading for the sitting room, where at least the chairs were more comfortable and the lighting wasn't so unforgiving.

Musical rooms, she thought. Just as well there weren't many in her house or they could be doing this all night, or at least until she said what she had to say and then chucked him out.

She didn't switch on the overhead light. Instead she turned on the lamp on the side table and then tucked herself into her favourite chair, an old, comfy thing that had witnessed her weep in front of many a sad movie.

'I don't know how we landed up here, Rafael,' she said slowly, watching as he made himself comfortable on a chair that was too small for him, 'but it's all wrong. We belong in different places. Good Lord, we even *live* in completely different countries!'

'Yes, you're right, we do.'

'And we should never, ever have got involved with one another.'

'Which just goes to show that fate is alive and doing well.'

'No, it doesn't. It just shows that we started something we should have known we would never finish.'

'Why?'

'Why what? Why did we start it? Because…well…and that's another thing! You started something because you wanted to find out more about me and my intentions and I started it because I ended up being attracted to you.

'But what we should have done was pay attention to the fact that really, together, we made no sense. I mean…' She rooted around for the most effective way she could think of to express what she was trying to say… 'You're talking absolute rubbish.' He stood up and pulled his chair over to her so that he was up close and personal and they were no longer divided by the width of the room. Now, he could actually *see* her in the dim, mellow lighting, could actually *touch* her if he wanted to. Much better.

Amy opened her mouth to object and he covered it with his hand. 'You've had your turn, now it's mine. Agreed?'

She nodded and he removed his hand.

'For me,' Rafael said quietly, 'the only thing that *doesn't* make sense is my life when you're not in it.' He was walking the sharp edge of a precipice and he didn't care. It was liberating to talk. He didn't understand how he could have doubted his ability to reveal himself to this woman because now he was finding it the easiest thing in the world to do. He reached out, searching for her hand, his eyes still firm on her face, and grasped it in his own.

'We've been over all that business of when we first met, the stupidity of not telling you who I was. But that seems irrelevant to me now. The relevant thing, the life-changing thing for me, was how you made me feel. I met you and I began to see the world, my life, *me,* in a different way. Do you understand what I'm saying?'

'No, could you explain further?' Amy was scared of blinking just in case this magical moment vanished in a puff of smoke.

Rafael smiled, amused. 'Only if you're sure I'm not boring you…'

'Oh, no—' Amy cleared her throat and tried to maintain her equilibrium '—it's good for men to show their feelings. Real men cry.'

'Hmm. Not sure about that…what I *am* sure about is that I misread the obvious when we met. Instead of asking myself how it was that you made me act out of character, I kidded myself that it didn't matter. When I flew over here to see you, I didn't stop to think how a simple case of lust could affect me so badly. If I had, I might have arrived at my conclusion earlier…'

'Conclusion?' Amy asked hopefully.

Rafael looked down at his fingers entwined with hers. 'I thought I wanted you, I thought we had unfinished business, but only in the physical sense. That was why I went back to Elizabeth. I was determined to give it another try because I was adamant that what I felt for her had to be more significant than what I felt for you. After all, on paper, she was my perfect match. Which brings me back to what you said about us making no sense together. On paper, we might not, but then love doesn't obey any written rules, does it?'

'Love?' Amy squeaked.

'Isn't love what this is all about?' Rafael looked at her and then touched the side of her face with his hand. 'I fell in love with you, Amy. You took my ordered, controlled,

predictable life and turned it upside down. I finished with
Elizabeth when I realised that I couldn't go on lying to
myself and then I came over here to tell you that I can't live
without you. I…I'm taking a gamble that you…feel the
same way about me.'

'And that must be very hard,' she murmured, 'because
you're not a gambler by nature.'

Suddenly, it was as if she had spent her life standing in the
middle of a storm that was now over. Her thoughts were very
clear. 'But you're not taking a gamble,' she said in a low
voice. 'Of course I love you, my darling. I mean…' she
couldn't resist a reluctant grin '…I know I do things on the
spur of the moment, but there's no way I would ever have
come to your office just because I was interested in your
body. Not,' she added, 'that it's not a very nice body.'

'Then perhaps you'd like to be a bit closer to this very nice
body on that very nice sofa over there, which would be a damn
sight more comfortable than me perching over you…'

'But no touching,' Amy told him, when they were lying,
entwined, on her sofa, which had not been fashioned to accommodate two people in a horizontal position, hence the fact
that she was half on top of him and his feet were sticking over
the side, 'at least not until we talk about…what happens next.
I know you have a problem with commitment but—'

'But that was then and this is now.' Rafael let his lips linger
on hers, tasting her sweetness and knowing, with deep
pleasure, that he would soon be tasting more than just her
mouth. It felt like coming home. 'And as for what happens
next…it's time for James and I to do a swap, by which I mean
that my brother could charm New York with his dazzling advertising skills and I could take London by the horns and
really get going on those ideas I've been putting together.'

'You mean you would move over here…*for me*?'

'For *us*…after all, husbands and wives do tend to share the same country.'

'Now I'm going to cry,' Amy whispered, her eyes filling up. 'You know what I'm like…'

Emotional, feisty, soft and very, very feminine. He smiled, his heart filled with a deep, unconditional love.

'So I take it that that's a *yes*…?'

'Yes, yes, yes, yes and *yes*! Oh, God. This is so wonderful!' She inundated him with kisses. 'I can't wait for you to make an honest woman of me! And in the meantime…'

'Let's see how a dishonest woman shows her love for her man…'

* * * * *

THE ROYAL HOUSE OF NIROLI
Always passionate, always proud

The richest royal family in the world—
united by blood and passion,
torn apart by deceit and desire

Nestled in the azure blue of the Mediterranean Sea, the majestic island of Niroli has prospered for centuries. The Fierezza men have worn the crown with passion and pride since ancient times. But now, as the king's health declines, and his two sons have been tragically killed, the crown is in jeopardy.

The clock is ticking—a new heir must be found before the king is forced to abdicate. By royal decree the internationally scattered members of the Fierezza family are summoned to claim their destiny. But any person who takes the throne must do so according to The Rules of the Royal House of Niroli. Soon secrets and rivalries emerge as the descendents of this ancient royal line vie for position and power. Only a true Fierezza can become ruler—a person dedicated to their country, their people...and their eternal love!

Each month starting in July 2007,
Harlequin Presents is delighted to bring you
an exciting installment from
THE ROYAL HOUSE OF NIROLI,
in which you can follow the epic search
for the true Nirolian king.
Eight heirs, eight romances, eight fantastic stories!

Here's your chance to enjoy a sneak preview of the first book delivered to you by royal decree...

FIVE minutes later she was standing immobile in front of the study's window, her original purpose of coming in forgotten, as she stared in shocked horror at the envelope she was holding. Waves of heat followed by icy chill surged through her body. She could hardly see the address now through her blurred vision, but the crest on its left-hand front corner stood out, its *royal* crest, followed by the address: *HRH Prince Marco of Niroli...*

She didn't hear Marco's key in the apartment door, she didn't even hear him calling out her name. Her shock was so great that nothing could penetrate it. It encased her in a kind of bubble, which only concentrated the torment of what she was suffering and branded it on her brain so that it could never be forgotten. It was only finally pierced by the sudden opening of the study door as Marco walked in.

"Welcome home, *Your Highness*. I suppose I ought to curtsy." She waited, praying that he would laugh and tell her that she had got it all wrong, that the envelope she was holding, addressing him as Prince Marco of Niroli, was some silly mistake. But like a tiny candle flame shivering vulnerably in the dark, her hope trembled fearfully. And then the look in Marco's eyes extinguished it as cruelly as a hand placed callously over a dying person's face to stem their last breath.

"Give that to me," he demanded, taking the envelope from her.

"It's too late, Marco," Emily told him brokenly. "I know the truth now…." She dug her teeth in her lower lip to try to force back her own pain.

"You had no right to go through my desk," Marco shot back at her furiously, full of loathing at being caught off-guard and forced into a position in which he was in the wrong, making him determined to find something he could accuse Emily of. "I trusted you…."

Emily could hardly believe what she was hearing. "No, you didn't trust me, Marco, and you didn't trust me because you knew that I couldn't trust you. And you knew that because you're a liar, and liars don't trust people because they know that they themselves cannot be trusted." She not only felt sick, she also felt as though she could hardly breathe. "You are Prince Marco of Niroli…. How could you not tell me who you are and still live with me as intimately as we have lived together?" she demanded brokenly.

"Stop being so ridiculously dramatic," Marco demanded fiercely. "You are making too much of the situation."

"*Too much?*" Emily almost screamed the words at him. "When were you going to tell me, Marco? Perhaps you just planned to walk away without telling me anything? After all, what do my feelings matter to you?"

"Of course they matter." Marco stopped her sharply. "And it was in part to protect them, and you, that I decided not to inform you when my grandfather first announced that he intended to step down from the throne and hand it on to me."

"To protect me?" Emily nearly choked on her fury. "Hand on the throne? No wonder you told me when you first took me to bed that all you wanted was sex. You *knew* that was the only kind of relationship there could ever be between us! You *knew* that one day you would be Niroli's king. No doubt you are expected to marry a princess. Is she picked out for you already, your *royal* bride?"

* * * * *

Look for THE FUTURE KING'S PREGNANT MISTRESS
by Penny Jordan in July 2007,
from Harlequin Presents,
available wherever books are sold.

HARLEQUIN *Presents*

THE ROYAL HOUSE OF NIROLI

Always passionate, always proud.

**The richest royal family in the world—
a family united by blood and passion,
torn apart by deceit and desire.**

Step into the glamorous, enticing world of the
Nirolian Royal Family. As the king ails he must find an
heir…each month an exciting new installment follows
the epic search for the true Nirolian king. Eight heirs,
eight romances, eight fantastic stories!

It's time for playboy prince Marco Fierezza to
claim his rightful place…on the throne of Niroli!
Emily loves Marco, but she has no idea he's a royal
prince! What will this king-in-waiting do when he
discovers his mistress is pregnant?

THE FUTURE KING'S PREGNANT MISTRESS

by Penny Jordan

(#2643)

On sale July 2007.

www.eHarlequin.com

HARLEQUIN®

Mediterranean NIGHTS™

Tycoon Elias Stamos is launching his newest luxury cruise ship from his home port in Greece. But someone from his past is eager to expose old secrets and to see the Stamos empire crumble.

Mediterranean Nights
launches in June 2007 with...

FROM RUSSIA, WITH LOVE
by *Ingrid Weaver*

Join the guests and crew of *Alexandra's Dream* as they are drawn into a world of glamour, romance and intrigue in this new 12-book series.

REQUEST YOUR FREE BOOKS!

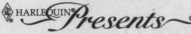

2 FREE NOVELS PLUS 2 FREE GIFTS!

PASSION GUARANTEED SEDUCTION

YES! Please send me 2 FREE Harlequin Presents® novels and my 2 FREE gifts. After receiving them, if I don't wish to receive any more books, I can return the shipping statement marked "cancel." If I don't cancel, I will receive 6 brand-new novels every month and be billed just $3.80 per book in the U.S., or $4.47 per book in Canada, plus 25¢ shipping and handling per book and applicable taxes, if any*. That's a savings of close to 15% off the cover price! I understand that accepting the 2 free books and gifts places me under no obligation to buy anything. I can always return a shipment and cancel at any time. Even if I never buy another book from Harlequin, the two free books and gifts are mine to keep forever.

106 HDN EEXK   306 HDN EEXV

Name	(PLEASE PRINT)	
Address		Apt. #
City	State/Prov.	Zip/Postal Code

Signature (if under 18, a parent or guardian must sign)

Mail to the **Harlequin Reader Service®:**
IN U.S.A.: P.O. Box 1867, Buffalo, NY 14240-1867
IN CANADA: P.O. Box 609, Fort Erie, Ontario L2A 5X3

Not valid to current Harlequin Presents subscribers.

Want to try two free books from another line?
Call 1-800-873-8635 or visit www.morefreebooks.com.

* Terms and prices subject to change without notice. NY residents add applicable sales tax. Canadian residents will be charged applicable provincial taxes and GST. This offer is limited to one order per household. All orders subject to approval. Credit or debit balances in a customer's account(s) may be offset by any other outstanding balance owed by or to the customer. Please allow 4 to 6 weeks for delivery.

Your Privacy: Harlequin is committed to protecting your privacy. Our Privacy Policy is available online at www.eHarlequin.com or upon request from the Reader Service. From time to time we make our lists of customers available to reputable firms who may have a product or service of interest to you. If you would prefer we not share your name and address, please check here. ☐

HP07

**Two billionaires, one Greek, one Spanish—
will they claim their unwilling brides?**

Meet Sandor and Miguel, men who've taken all the prizes
when it comes to looks, power, wealth and arrogance.
Now they want marriage with two beautiful women.
But this time, for the first time, both Mediterranean
billionaires have met their matches and it will take more
than money or cool to tame their unwilling mistresses!

Miguel made Amber Taylor feel beautiful for the
first time. For Miguel it was supposed to be a
two-week affair…but now he'd taken the most
precious gift of all—her innocence!

TAKEN:
THE SPANIARD'S VIRGIN
Miguel's story (#2644)

by Lucy Monroe

On sale July 2007.